FOREWORD

When I first had the idea for BookShots, I knew that I wanted to include romantic stories. The whole point of BookShots is to give people lightning-fast reads that completely capture them for just a couple hours in their day—so publishing romance felt right.

I have a lot of respect for romance authors. I took a stab at the genre when I wrote *Suzanne's Diary for Nicholas* and *Sundays at Tiffany's*. While I was happy with the results, I learned that the process of writing those stories required hard work and dedication.

That's why I wanted to pair up with the best romance authors for BookShots. I work with writers who know how to draw emotions out of their characters, all while catapulting their plots forward.

The thing that impressed me most about *The Mating Season* was that Laurie Horowitz knew her character, Sophie Castle, inside and out. It was like she'd walked around in her skin. Horowitz looked into Sophie's professional passions and expertly aligned those traits with her personality, which brought her to life. And Sophie certainly meets her match in Rigg Greensman—you just wait and see.

James Patterson

THE
MATING
SEASON

Chapter 1

WHEN I GET off the plane in Sharm el-Sheikh, I feel like I've been sitting for hours in a trash compactor. The man beside me smelled strongly of garlic and fried food.

My mother says that flying used to be romantic. Not anymore. When I catch my reflection in an airport window, I see that over nineteen hours of air travel isn't exactly a beauty treatment. Not that I care too much about that. I am a scientist, an ornithologist, a bird nerd. I am here for the adventure of a lifetime, and I can turn this exhaustion into exhilaration. All it takes is a little resolve.

I remove my itinerary from the lower side pocket of my safari vest. I have two more copies of the schedule in my luggage. I printed out three just in case something happened to one—or two—of them. The sheet of paper clearly indicates that a driver is supposed to be here to pick me up.

I go off to find my Patagonia at the luggage carousel. It's a new bag my mother gave me for this trip, a lime-green water-resistant rolling duffle. My mother wanted to buy me a Tumi, but I lobbied for the Patagonia. What self-respecting outdoorswoman would pick a Tumi over a Patagonia? My mother calls it my *Patagucci*, because it's expensive for what it is. She knows about these things. She's been in retail since my father died when I was four.

I am thrown by my missing driver. There's no sign saying SO-PHIE CASTLE anywhere to be found. Here I am in Egypt—my first time out of the United States. I could call Corey West, my producer at the Discovery Channel, or better yet, my friend Halley (named for the comet) who works with him and was the force behind getting me this gig. But no. I'm a big girl. I can figure out how to get from the airport to the hotel without calling Los Angeles.

The driver should have been here to pick up two of us: me and my cameraman, Rigg Greensman. He came to the Discovery Channel from *When Sharks Attack,* which aired on Nat Geo Wild, and he is supposed to be one of the best cameramen in the field. Halley says I was lucky to get him. I'm sure she's right, but it's a little hard to believe when he's not here. I googled him before I left the United States and printed out all the information I could find, including his picture. When I showed it to my mother, she said, "He's too handsome for his own good." I don't understand that expression since he probably benefits from those looks, while any girl in his general vicinity is likely to be struck down by them. Anyone but me. I don't pick up the shiny pebbles on the beach. I take the ones that are weirdly colored or oddly shaped. In a choice between Shrek and Prince Charming, I'd choose Shrek. Rigg, with his sun-kissed curls and cleft chin, looks too much like a drawing of a prince.

Finally, I go outside and grab a taxi. The cabbie doesn't speak much English, and all I know how to say in Arabic is *As-Salaam-alaikum*. This driver could take me anywhere. I'm at his mercy. I take my compass out of the left upper pocket of my safari vest. At least we are going in the right direction: south. If we were going north, we'd be heading toward Israel. Because I don't know how long the journey is supposed to be, I can't relax. The time ticks by and we get farther and farther from the bright lights of Sharm el-Sheikh. The only thing that comforts me is that I am hardly the type of woman who gets kidnapped into white slavery. I cut my long hair infrequently and when I do, I cut it with nail scissors. I don't have a unibrow, but fifteen minutes with a pair of tweezers would not go amiss. My teeth are straight, thanks to my mother who has made every sacrifice to make sure I've had the best of everything, including braces. My breasts aren't much to speak of, not that anyone's been speaking much of them lately. My eyes are a greenish-brown. When you take all the features separately, each is attractive enough, but with the way I manage them—or fail to manage them—they don't cause men to trail after me like lovesick puppies. Not that I'd want them to.

After almost an hour, dusk has turned to darkness and we pull into the gravel parking lot of the Pigeon House. The stucco exterior makes the building look like a sand dune and I feel a little like Lawrence of Arabia. I pay the driver in Egyptian pounds, glad that I had the foresight to get them, and walk inside, dragging my bag behind me.

Chapter 2

WHEN I FIND my driver and cameraman, they are sitting at a plastic table in the bar at the back of the Pigeon House. I don't know whether I am relieved or furious.

"You were supposed to wait for me," I say, stabbing at my itinerary.

"And hello to you, too," Rigg says. He stands and sticks out his hand. It isn't until I reach out my own hand that I realize my fingernails are dirty. I pull it back. Rigg probably thinks I'm snubbing him. "Have a seat. This is our driver and translator, Ahmed," Rigg says. In his buttery leather jacket, Rigg looks much as I expected he would. His Ray-Bans hold his floppy hair off his forehead like a woman's headband.

"Hello, Ahmed. Didn't you read the itinerary?" I sit down in the kind of plastic chair you can pick up at Walmart, three for ten dollars.

Ahmed looks at me blankly. He obviously doesn't understand the word *itinerary* so I take it out and wave it in his face.

"Put that thing away, will you?" Rigg says. His tone makes me feel like a guy who has just opened his raincoat and flashed his junk.

I sit down and look at the menu. It's in both English and Arabic. Turns out that the Middle East is a vegetarian's paradise. I don't eat birds, of course. After I stopped eating them, it was only a short jump to not eating anything sentient. I order falafel.

When the food comes, I tuck in. I haven't had anything to eat for five hours. I focus on the food and block out everything else. That is, until I feel Rigg staring at me. I pause to look up.

"Haven't you ever seen a girl eat before?" I ask, wiping some tahini off my chin with a paper napkin.

"Not quite like that," he says.

"The girls you date probably don't eat," I say.

"I don't know why you would say that," he says.

"Just a hunch." I look toward the bar and beckon over our translator.

"What do you need?" Ahmed asks. He has very short cropped hair, bronze skin, and green eyes. He couldn't be much older than twenty.

"I'd like a beer," I say.

He calls out to a blond girl behind the bar. "Katya, this lady would like a beer," he says in English.

"I could have done that," I say.

"But I'm your translator." He smiles. His two front teeth overlap just enough to be appealing.

I take a breath and look at Rigg. "Tell me a little about your-self," I say.

"What do you want to know?" He leans back on the two rear legs of his chair and I'm tempted to tell him he'll break his neck if he doesn't come back down to earth.

"What got you interested in birds?" I ask.

"I'm not interested in birds," he says.

He's been put on this bird project. He could at least pretend to be interested in birds.

"Oh," I say.

"I've spent the last few years working on *When Sharks Attack*," he says.

"So how'd you end up here?"

"Just a little careless mistake." He is wobbling on that chair now. "My assistant lost his little finger."

"Lost it?"

"Well, a shark ate it. We were trying to get an impossible shot," he says.

"I suppose it could have been worse," I say. "It could have been his whole hand or his thumb, which is much more useful than a little finger." I shovel up some hummus with a piece of pita and take a bite. "So, this is basically a demotion for you."

"I wouldn't call it that," he says without conviction.

"Well, who knows? You could end up liking birds."

His expression says that I shouldn't count on it, but he gives me a crooked smile.

I wipe my plate clean with a piece of bread.

"They won't even have to wash that," Rigg says.

"I hope they do." I get up and stand for a moment with my hands on my hips. "I'm going to bed and I suggest you do the same. Early day tomorrow. And just in case you haven't read the itinerary, we start at dawn."

Chapter 3

RIGG STRETCHED OUT on his bed. He shouldn't have had so much to drink. He was thoroughly pissed. Arak is powerful stuff. Rigg loved the taste of licorice and even though this licorice burned going down, he drank four glasses.

That girl he's supposed to work with is what you'd call a *hot mess*. What was in that nest of hair? He saw a bunch of clips holding it up, but worried there were other creatures lurking inside. Hadn't she ever heard of a hairbrush? And that safari vest is ridiculous.

The Pigeon House is a dive. A cockroach the size of his thumb came crawling out of the sink while he was brushing his teeth. The shower is in the corner of the room and isn't delineated from the rest of the place with a door or a curtain. It's just a showerhead with a drain and a gutter.

Rigg would like to blame someone else for his predicament, but he knew that it was his fault. He had used the word *careless* to describe his behavior on *When Sharks Attack,* but the correct word was *reckless*. Rigg had fostered a reputation for getting all the best shark footage. He was hoping that would help him get into directing. He wanted to direct a feature film, but he would be happy to start with an advert. Advertising could be sexy. A good spot could capture an agent's attention. Lots of directors were discovered that way. Rigg's ambition earned him a reputation for being egotistical and difficult to work with. That's what the exec at Nat Geo said when they let him go. Rigg was grateful the guy hadn't mentioned the finger.

Rigg knew he'd been lucky to get this assignment. The money was respectable. He'd be working with a scientist on a prestige project—*boring*, but *prestige*. To him, those words are synonymous. When Rigg was growing up, he'd watched enough boring documentaries on the BBC with his father to last a lifetime. *The aardvark is a burrowing, nocturnal animal usually found in Africa. It sleeps in the heat of the day, but awakes at night to claw through mounds of dirt for its favorite food: termites.* Now, if that same aardvark were to be eaten by lions, the show would be worth watching. The worst thing about those kinds of nature films was that they weren't dramatic enough. That's why sharks and grizzlies would always beat out birds.

Rigg got up. He'd better drink some water and take a couple of paracetamol. Was the water all right to drink here? He probably should have asked. There were two bottles near the sink. Maybe he should have used one of them to brush his teeth. Too late now.

He opened his backpack, took out *People* magazine, and flipped through it looking for that picture of Nicola he liked. The stunning Nicola Upton. Supposedly, she was dating her agent now.

Nicola and Rigg had been on-again, off-again since university, when he, she, Simon, and Philip had all been starting out together. Now, Nicola was being called the next Emma Thompson; Simon, the next Julian Fellowes; and Philip, the next Hugh Laurie—all alumni of the Cambridge Footlights. And what was Rigg? Rigg Greensman was the next big nothing.

His father would say Rigg was wallowing. Rigg's father, Sir Alastair Greensman, was not fond of wallowing. He believed it was not very British. Sir Alastair was disappointed by Rigg's choice of profession. The Greensman men always went into law and then politics.

By now, Rigg had hoped he could have presented Sir Alastair with a BAFTA or an Academy Award. But, no, he was here on the Sinai Peninsula to film birds. The irony was that his father probably would respect this project more than any of Rigg's glitzier jobs.

Rigg traced his finger over the picture of Nicola's face. She'd been his first love. It had been ten years since they'd left university, and they both had had plenty of growing to do. Nicola's success came early, and with it, came a desire to spread her wings. Rigg didn't spend their time apart moping. He dated one actress-slash-model after another. Sophie Castle had pegged him there. But his playboy lifestyle didn't mean he was not a serious person. He'd settle down someday. Probably with Nicola. And that was one of the reasons he was here. Nicola was starring in *Nefertiti,* which was being filmed in Sharm el-Sheikh, less than an hour away.

Chapter 4

"WHERE'S RIGG?" I ask as I get into Ahmed's tattered Subaru wagon.

"I come back for him," Ahmed says. "I drop you first."

I am not crazy about that idea, but I don't want to get off on the wrong foot. We drive into Ras Mohammed National Park while it's still dark. I have done my research and found the perfect spot. Ahmed and I unload the equipment, and Ahmed drives away, leaving me alone on a small promontory overlooking the Gulf of Aqaba. My eyes become accustomed to the dark. Many people seek out the romance of sunsets, but I favor sunrises. It's when the world is waking up and everything feels full of possibility. The good thing about birds, maybe all animals, is that they live in the present. When I'm with them, so do I. I love a desert wilderness. Wide-open spaces make it easier for me to breathe.

I wait.

The sunrise is spectacular and just as the pink is turning to orange and the orange is becoming blue, a flock of white storks lifts up and streaks across the sky.

It would make a great shot, a wonderful shot, but Rigg is not here to take it.

I wait some more. Near the water, the ruffs, a cousin of the sandpiper, are running all over the place. A ruff, like many bird species, is sexually dimorphic. The male is the pretty one and the female is plain. These birds are named for the male's ruff of feathers around his neck.

Their mating ritual, like that of other birds, is called *lekking*. Even the word for their mating sounds absurd. The male is so cocky, demonstrative, and self-satisfied. He flutters toward the female and attempts to stir up some action by displaying his glorious good looks. When that fails, he flutters over and jumps on his beloved. The males can get pretty aggressive with each other as they compete for a female, too. It's hilarious, and I find it endlessly entertaining.

I would have been fine with just being out there alone watching these miraculous birds if I weren't responsible for putting together enough film to make a kick-ass documentary about migratory birds in the next eight days. There was no guarantee that the shots we missed this morning would ever come again. In fact, the only guarantee was that those particular moments were gone forever.

My bird journal (it contains my *life list*, a list of every bird I've ever seen) usually calms me down so I take it out to record what I've seen. Osprey. Heron. Tern. I draw a ruff and give it sunglasses and a leather jacket like Rigg's. I make a bubble coming out of its mouth that says, "I am a loser with an ego the size of a circus tent."

I do like to anthropomorphize my birds. It's fun to give them personalities and make them seem a little human, but this tendency is something I keep to myself because I wouldn't want anyone to think I wasn't a serious scientist. I hear a deep rumble in the distance and stand to see Ahmed's Subaru thundering toward me. It stops at my makeshift encampment and both Ahmed and Rigg climb out of the car. Ahmed starts to unload all of Rigg's equipment.

I'm an outdoorswoman, so I can tell time by the sun, but I want Rigg to know that I know he's late without having to say anything. It's a tactic of my mother's, so I give it a try by pulling my watch out of a small pocket in my vest and giving it a pointed look.

My mother, apparently, has more self-control than I do. "You were supposed to be here two hours ago," I say. "What is it about *the crack of dawn* that you didn't understand?" I am not crazy about how shrill my voice sounds. The knots in my shoulders are probably having baby knots.

"I wasn't feeling too well," Rigg says.

"Whose fault is that?" I feel like such a harpy that I can barely stand myself, but this guy has to know who's boss.

"I have one thing to say." He begins to set up his tripod.

"What?"

"Don't drink the water."

"I think you're confusing water with alcohol."

"I don't know if I can stand to be treated with such tenderness." Rigg sounds both snarky and resigned.

"You missed at least two fabulous opportunities. The storks migrating and the ruffs lekking. This may not be important to you, but it's extremely important to me."

Rigg stares at me as if I'm speaking in a foreign tongue. "Life's ruff," he finally says.

"You do know that puns are the lowest form of wit?" I say, taking a step toward him.

His midnight-blue eyes are bloodshot. "Even the lowest form of wit is better than none at all."

He turns away to finish setting up his cameras.

He might as well not have bothered. The rest of the day is a dud. When I get back to my room, I stomp around in such a fury that the chaos of lekking looks repressed by comparison.

Chapter 5

ONE DAY GONE and nothing has been accomplished. It's not as if we had all the time in the world. Seven days is barely enough. I'm not going to let this entitled Brit screw up my chance of a lifetime, but I can't call LA yet since it's ten hours earlier there. They still have the time we've just wasted.

I thought when they put this "big talent" on my project, it meant they were taking me seriously. Instead, I find out that they were pawning off a bad-boy cameraman on the one person who would be too naive to understand.

The shower in my room is not enclosed by glass or anything resembling a partition. It's just a showerhead, a drain, and a gutter to keep the water from getting all over the room. I've never seen anything like it. I close the window shades and get undressed. I don't bother to unclip my hair. I just shove a shower cap over it. I fiddle with the knobs under the showerhead. Even though this is a shoddy hotel in the desert, the spray gushes out. I close my eyes and let the pounding water rinse away the dust and tension.

When I open my eyes, Rigg is standing inside the door of my room. He looks as shocked as I feel. I grab for the towel hanging from a nearby hook and try to cover myself with one hand while turning off the water with the other.

"I thought you said 'Come in,'" Rigg says.

"I can guarantee that I certainly did not." The bit of material that I am trying to cover myself with is hardly big enough to merit the name *towel*. It's only about four times the size of a washcloth and offers less coverage than ostrich feathers give a fan dancer.

"Why didn't you lock your door?" Rigg raises his voice as if I were the one who had committed the massive faux pas. He keeps looking at me. It's more of a glare than a leer, but he does have the option of looking away, and he doesn't take it.

"Why am I not shocked that you're blaming me for your mistake?" I ask.

"And why am I not shocked that you'd try to put me in the wrong before covering yourself up properly?"

He has no shame, this guy.

"You don't have to keep looking. You could turn around." I am still standing there as if in the final stages of a striptease. I'm getting goosebumps. And he is still staring.

"You really don't understand men at all, do you?"

"I don't understand you. That's for sure."

I sidle over to my bathrobe and shrug into it, using the arm that isn't holding the poor excuse for a towel.

"Can you close your eyes or something?" I ask.

"I'd rather not." His laughter is a low rumble. If he's trying to make me feel vulnerable, he's doing a damned good job. Screw it. I toss away the towel with a flourish as I snuggle into my favorite robe. It took up so much room in my suitcase that I had to leave some extra underwear and T-shirts behind, but now I'm so glad I did. This thick terry cloth feels like a fortress.

"You're no gentleman," I say.

"I'm decimated," he says, pressing his lips together as if he can barely contain a snicker.

"Did you have a reason for invading my privacy?" I ask.

"I came to ask you if you wanted to have a drink. We could try to bury the hatchet."

I'll bury it in your head, I think. "As you can see, I'm not dressed."

"You could get dressed," he says.

"With you watching?"

"You could always dress in the toilet stall."

"It's too small."

"Maybe you rushed in the shower as soon as you saw me coming. You probably like being looked at." He walks toward me and I take a step back toward the wall.

"I would have had to run across the room naked." I wrap my arms across my chest.

"Well, sorry about the interruption," he says, stepping back. He doesn't look sorry. His lip is twisted in a supercilious curl; he thinks he has the upper hand.

*　　*　　*

When he's gone, I pick up my recorder from the nightstand. I play a treble recorder and no, it's not just for kids. Plenty of grown-ups play this versatile instrument. In honor of my trip, I've been learning a tune from *Scheherazade* by Nikolai Rimsky-Korsakov. Such a beautiful, plaintive melody, but instead of helping me unwind, it makes me think of Scheherazade and how she had to tell the sultan stories to keep him interested enough not to lop off her head in the morning. Men!

I am in no mood to run into Rigg at the bar, so I ask Katya if she can bring me something to eat. I'll wait here until it's time to call LA. I don't want to give my fury a chance to dissipate. When she knocks on the door about a half hour later, she has brought me a falafel sandwich and a bottle of water.

"What is that ugly hat?" she asks, pointing to my head. It is then I realize that I'm still wearing my shower cap.

"It's to keep my hair dry," I say, pulling it off and throwing it into the corner.

"Some things are just too ugly to wear," Katya says.

"It's functional. And, besides, no one else was supposed to see it."

"I saw it. That is one person too many."

And Rigg has seen it, too. So what if I look like someone's grandmother in it? It's just a shower cap.

*　　*　　*

I eat my dinner and read *Living Bird* while I wait to Skype with Corey West. There is an article about penguins in Antarctica. The writer calls it a penguin revolution, but really it's an article about how penguins are changing their behavior due to global warming. This is just the kind of thing I'd want to expose on film. I applaud this writer, but let's face it, only a handful of ornithologists are likely to read her piece, no matter how well intentioned it is. I want to reach more people than that. These stories mean life and death to the ecosystem, and this idiot Rigg Greensman can't even be bothered to wake up on time to record them.

When Corey West flicks on his video, he is holding a cup of steaming coffee. "What's up, Sophie? Everything okay?" Corey is cheerful. Maybe he has forgotten that I can see him because he is flipping through papers with the hand that's not holding the coffee. "How are you and Rigg getting along?"

"To be honest, we're not. He didn't even show up this morning. Wasted the whole day. I don't think he's serious about this. Was this his last stop before he was thrown out of the industry or something? Did you know that he caused a guy to lose a finger?"

"Everyone knows that," Corey said.

"The man is a menace."

"Just be careful of your fingers. Keep them away from the birds' beaks." Corey almost sputters up his coffee at that one.

"It's not funny. Rigg Greensman is not behaving like a professional."

"And how professional is it to be ratting him out at the first sign of trouble?"

"Don't you want the film to be a success?" I ask.

"Of course I do. That's why I sent him. Look, doll, I've gotta wrap this up. I have a call sheet as long as my arm. My advice to you is to do the best you can with what you've got because you aren't getting anyone else." Corey flicks at something in his nose with his thumb.

"I can see you," I say.

"Sorry. Why didn't you turn on your video?"

"I'm in my bathrobe."

"You probably look very nice in your bathrobe," he says.

"I'm not sure whether to feel flattered or sexually harassed."

He laughs.

"Now, stop whining and do the work. Remember why you are doing this. It's for the birds."

"Right," I say, taking a deep breath. "It's for the birds."

Chapter 6

RIGG WAS IN his room when he got the call from Corey West.

"Look, man," Corey said. "Don't screw this up. You can at least show up on time."

"She called you?"

"I *am* the producer. Rigg, I wasn't going to tell you this, but I gave you this job as a favor to your friend Philip."

Philip Piggott-Barnes could get anyone to do anything since he'd become the hugely popular star of the CBS drama *Contempt of Court*. It was kind of Philip to get Rigg this job, but it was also a blow to Rigg's ego, which, despite the impression he tried to give, was only about as thick as an eggshell at this point.

"Everyone knows you're good at what you do—maybe even the best—but no one wants to work with you. You have a reputation for being difficult," Corey said.

"I'm a perfectionist."

"A perfectionist with a bad attitude. Look, man, I'm going to give it to you straight. This might seem like an unimportant bird project to you, but if you handle it right, it's a chance to re-habilitate yourself."

"Sophie Castle is a hopeless twit."

"She may be inexperienced, but if you help instead of hinder her, you'll be doing yourself a big favor."

After Rigg hung up, he paced the room. He wondered if he should call Philip to thank him or leave it alone. The last time they had been together, they were having coffee at Kings Road in West Hollywood. Everyone who passed looked at Philip and it wasn't just that he was famous. Philip Piggott-Barnes had that indefinable something that drew eyes wherever he went.

A mercy gig. Bollocks.

Rigg needed a drink.

Unfortunately, the first person he saw when he entered the bar was Sophie. She was alone at a table nursing a beer. He sat down without asking her if she wanted company. The image of her naked body was affixed to the inside of his eyelids.

"I'll bet you were a tattletale in school," he said. Sophie didn't answer. She grimaced and looked at the bottle in her hand. "You're going to get a big vertical wrinkle between your eyes if you keep frowning like that."

"I don't care. I'm a scientist, not a fashion model," she said.

"Don't worry, bird nerd. No one would ever mistake you for a fashion model," Rigg said. Sophie upended the bottle into her mouth and guzzled, as if to prove she really didn't care about her image. "You shouldn't have called Corey West."

"I'm sorry, but I don't want my project ruined by a guy who thinks the sun shines out of his ass."

"You don't go talking rubbish about your associates. That's not how the game is played."

"It wasn't rubbish; it was the truth."

"Your version." He gestured for a drink. "And why did you come to the bar in your pajamas?"

"These aren't pajamas. They're scrubs."

"But you're wearing them as pajamas, aren't you?"

"They're comfortable and they don't take up much room in my suitcase."

"Scrubs should be worn by doctors and maybe nurses, preferably in a hospital."

"I'll alert the media." Sophie said. Then, she got up and walked out of the bar.

Rigg sipped his arak. He'd have to stick to one drink. It wouldn't do to get drunk. He couldn't mess up again.

About five minutes later, Rigg heard a melody. It sounded like it was being carried on the wind. You didn't have an education like Rigg's without being able to *name that classical tune.* It was from Rimsky-Korsakov's *Scheherazade* Opus 35.

The king in that story got a bad rap. The man had been hurt; his beloved wife was unfaithful. Rigg had to admit that killing most of the maidens in the kingdom was an overreaction. But the story had always made some kind of twisted sense to him.

Chapter 7

THE NEXT MORNING, I feel vaguely ashamed. It could be because Rigg had seen me naked. But I know there's nothing shameful about the human body. It's natural. I think what is really bothering me is the way he called me a tattletale. He hit the nail right on the head with that one. In school, you could count on me to turn kids in for cheating. Rigg Greensman thinks I'm a weird nerd, and I think he's an arrogant jerk. And I still have to pull up my socks and make this work.

Ahmed drives us both out to Ras Mohammed in the morning. Rigg gets in front and I sit in the back with the equipment.

"Lovely morning," Ahmed says.

We each grunt our replies and look out of our respective windows. It's a beautiful day and the sun is just rising. As we unload our supplies, it is silent, but for the birds chirping.

"Do you still need me?" Ahmed asks after we have unpacked everything.

"Could you please come back to get us at four?" I ask.

"That's ten hours," Rigg says.

"I can count."

"Come back at two, Ahmed," Rigg says.

Instead of losing my temper, I take a deep breath. "How about three o'clock? We'll compromise."

Rigg nods. I've let him see that his opinion matters, even though I don't think it does. It's a management technique, and managing him is essential if I want to make a good film. I sit cross-legged on a flat rock near the water's edge. Rigg sits down beside me.

"What do we do now?" he asks.

"We wait."

"For what?"

"For something to happen." Then, as if I've orchestrated it, a group of sandpipers appear and start running back and forth along the shoreline. "Like that," I say, pointing to the birds.

"You want me to film that?" He sounds incredulous, as if I am asking him to make a movie of toast popping from a toaster. In fact, from his tone, I think he'd be more interested in the toast.

"I can lay in some commentary later," I say.

"Like what? 'Here are some birds running back and forth.'"

"Don't you think they're funny?"

"Ricky Gervais is funny. These birds? Not so much."

"Wait until you see the ruffs. They are hilarious. They remind me a little of you."

"I don't think I'm hilarious."

I don't bother to lower my voice since the sandpipers aren't likely to be frightened away by a little noise. Even if they are, they are fairly common, and we'll have plenty of opportunities to film them.

"With the ruffs, the male is the pretty one. The female is drab by comparison."

"Is that supposed to be a compliment?" Rigg asks.

"And ruffs are conceited."

"You're making that up. How can a bird be conceited?"

"Trust me. They can."

"I'm not conceited," he says loudly. The birds fly away. "If I were really as self-important as you seem to think I am, would I be serving as the entire crew on a bird documentary with a girl who knows nothing whatsoever about entertainment?"

"I don't think you have a choice," I say, standing up. "Besides, this isn't about entertainment. We're informing the public."

"That's where you're wrong. Haven't you ever heard 'A spoonful of sugar helps the medicine go down'?"

"Are you actually quoting Mary Poppins to me?"

"How about, 'You can catch more flies with honey than with vinegar'?"

"I don't want to catch flies."

"You want an audience, don't you?"

"Of course."

He stands up and rests his hands on his hips. "Well, the cold hard fact is that hardly anyone is going to see your bird documentary."

"If I can change the mind of even one person…" I say, jutting out my chin like Sally Field in *Norma Rae*.

"I suppose that would depend on the person," Rigg says and shakes his head. He walks back toward his tripod and fiddles with his cameras.

"Look," I whisper. "It's a greater painted-snipe." A long-billed bird dances through the swamp to our left. Then it lifts its large wings and launches itself into the sky. I follow it, not just with my eyes, but with my spirit. When my consciousness returns to earth, Rigg is staring at me.

"What?" I ask.

"You were transfixed," he says as if he's never seen anyone fully engaged in their work.

"That's what I want to share," I say.

"Then you have to do something about it. I know about this. I went to university with Philip Piggott-Barnes and Simon Marsten. I know about entertainment. They're my closest friends. If you want to share what you know, you've got to engage your audience."

"Philip Piggott-Barnes is famous."

"Yeah."

"Do you want to be famous?"

"Fame is the happy side effect of doing something well," he says.

"Says who?"

"Me."

"Oh, that seemed like a quote. I guess that sounds good, but it's not true. Even the best ornithologist in the world is not likely to ever be famous." I hop off my rock to stretch my legs. "So, do you want to be famous?"

"Doesn't everyone?"

"No. There are many things that are more important than fame and glory," I say.

He looks at me as if he's waiting for me to name one.

Chapter 8

IF I DON'T manage to interest Rigg in birds, this project isn't going to come together. I'm in a panic. If I can't get him to see what I see, how am I going to show it to anyone else? Yesterday, we saw a few birds, but the sights weren't exactly in league to turn this guy on—to the birds, I mean.

This morning, though, I'm in luck. The white storks are back. Their wings are edged in black and they have spindly red legs and yellow beaks. They are all facing in one direction like many little soldiers. Then, suddenly, they fly up and hundreds of wings fill the sky. In flight, it looks like the hand of a great giant has tossed black and white confetti.

When I look at Rigg, he is filming—thank God. There's an expression on his face I haven't seen before. The cynical look is gone, replaced by a look of absorption. I think this just might be the miracle I've been waiting for. When the storks fly off and the sky is empty, I say, "You'd have to be dead not to find that awesome."

"Watch out. Your passion is showing," he says.

"I'm not embarrassed by that. Everyone needs to be passionate about something. I wish I could make you see what I see."

"You can't make me, but you can help me. You can guide me. It isn't just me you need to help. You need to do that for your entire audience."

"But the birds speak for themselves."

"Actually, they don't. You only think that because they speak to you. Look, it is one thing to relay dry, scientific facts from behind the camera. It's another thing to light someone's fire." He walks toward me until he is standing so close that I can smell the minty toothpaste on his breath. Just as he comes near enough to kiss—not that I'm thinking of kissing him—he turns away abruptly. "The problem is your current narration. Let's face it; you could make armed robbery seem dull," he says as he adjusts one of his cameras. "Have you ever heard of infotainment?"

"Is it anything like a schnoodle?" I ask.

He looks at me and sighs. "What's a schnoodle?"

"It's a designer dog made by mixing two breeds that don't necessarily belong together."

"Information and entertainment are like fish and chips, tea and biscuits, mac and cheese."

"You hungry?"

"I'm trying to make a point here."

"I get it. I'm boring." It is something I suspected, which is probably why it bothers me so much to hear him say it.

"But you don't have to be." He looks through the camera at me. "You are not entirely unattractive."

"What does my level of attractiveness have to do with anything?"

"I want to see how you look on camera."

"Not a good idea."

"Just sit there on that stone and tell me about when you first fell in love with birds."

I am reluctant to do this, but I figure I have very little to lose except for my dignity, and most of that went when Rigg saw me naked and wearing a shower cap. I settle on a boulder.

"Just pretend I'm not here," Rigg says, as if that's possible. He is not the kind of presence that's easy to ignore. "Tell me about how you became a twitcher."

"It's birder."

"Birder, then."

"My mother signed me up for a bird walk at TreePeople when I was eight."

"What is TreePeople?"

"A foundation dedicated to conservation." I pause. I can't believe he's never heard of TreePeople. According to the internet, he's been living around LA for the last six years.

"Okay, continue."

"It was dark when my mother dropped me off that Saturday morning. She hadn't read the fine print. It was a bird walk for adults. My friend Halley's mother hadn't read the info carefully, either, or maybe neither of them cared. We were the only two kids there. Halley and I have been friends ever since. She works for Corey West."

"That's how you got this gig?"

"Yup. Anyway, Halley liked it well enough, but for me, it was electric. I've never been as happy as I was out there in the woods."

"Weren't you happy at home?"

"Happy enough. My mother had to work a lot and my dad died when I was four. And as you were so perspicacious to realize, I was nerdy and maybe a little lonely."

"I'm not sure you should use the word *perspicacious*. The general public might not understand it."

"But you understand it, don't you?"

"Of course."

"Well, I'm telling you, not the general public. And I think you make a mistake when you underestimate them." It's getting hot and I remove my vest. "Anyway, after that, I wanted to fly."

"But you were sad because you couldn't."

"No. I decided to make myself a pair of wings from some parachute material I found in the attic. It was my father's. He was a paratrooper. My first memory is of him jumping out of an airplane. His parachute was blue and yellow and red. It was like he was attached to an enormous balloon. It looked like flying to me."

"Did he die jumping out of a plane?"

"Walking across the street. He was run over by a car."

"That's awful."

"My mom always said that it is a lesson in how you shouldn't be afraid to take risks, because you just never know."

"What happened to the wings you made?"

"My mother confiscated them right before I jumped off the roof of our garage."

Rigg signals me to pause. "Okay, there are some birds over there," he says, still filming. "Walk toward them and explain what they are. Pretend you are with your friend Halley, and you're talking to her. Don't pay any attention to me."

Easier said than done. Still, I figure I can give it a try. I pad across the loose rocks toward the water.

"This is a brown booby," I say, gesturing toward it as if I'm Vanna White on *Wheel of Fortune.* "If we are patient, we might see him catch a fish in midair."

"How do you know it's a him?"

"Brown boobies are sexually dimorphic, like the ruffs. Lots of birds are. The male gets all the fancy feathers."

"Okay. Now, walk toward the camera and continue talking."

I move toward Rigg and pretend that I'm talking only to him. "In the booby's mating ritual, the males do an elaborate dance. He raises his feet alternately several times, and then he does what we in the ornithologist business call sky-pointing. He extends his wings toward his tail, raises his head, and lets out a long continuous whistle." I demonstrate using my arms as wings.

Then, I continue to move toward Rigg. "The early mariners named them boobies, because they thought the birds were stupid."

"Why was that?"

"Because the boobies weren't afraid of humans."

"Those early mariners may have had a point."

"If you ask me, it says more about the humans than the birds."

Rigg flips off the camera. "Well done, Sophie. You're a natural."

"I very much doubt that, but if you think it will improve the film, we can give this a try. After all, you're the one with the experience."

"So, you're finally willing to admit it."

"It's not an opinion; it's a fact. Whether I admit it or not has nothing to do with it."

I'm just glad that Rigg didn't act all juvenile when he heard the word *booby*.

This film might have a chance after all.

Chapter 9

"ARE YOU GOING to wear that?" Rigg asks as I step into the back of Ahmed's car. We are on our way to Sharm el-Sheikh, and I am wearing the same gear I have worn every day since I arrived. It has become increasingly obvious that Rigg Greensman thinks that women in burkas have more fashion sense than I do.

"To what exactly are you referring?" I ask.

"That many-pocketed vest. Do you have to wear it?"

"If I don't, how will I carry my wallet and other necessities?"

"There's a new invention. Perhaps you've heard of it. They call it a handbag."

"You don't carry one," I say.

"I'm a man."

"I don't see what difference that makes," I say.

"And therein lies the problem," Rigg says, but he laughs.

Ahmed starts the car. It takes almost an hour to get to Sharm. Ahmed stops at Il Mercato, a mall that reminds me of an out-door Caesars Palace in Las Vegas because it has the same inauthentic look. There is a curved pergola held up by Corinthian columns. The architect was trying to get at something, but I'm not sure what it was. He or she didn't stick to the ancient Mediterranean theme when choosing the street lamps; they look like rows of enormous lollipops.

The Starbucks calls out to Rigg, and we go in for a taste of home. After the three of us get our drinks, we take a table outside. I've never been much of a mall shopper. Indoor malls make me dizzy. I think it's the lighting. This shopping center is outdoors, and it's a pleasant seventy degrees. A soft breeze drifts toward us from the gulf. When we finish our coffees, we make a plan to meet up with Ahmed later and Rigg leads me away past a row of stores. He looks at each window display and finally chooses a shop. Rigg seems to have an instinct for shopping, something I find a little strange in such a rugged man. The guys I know hear the words *banana republic* and think of an unstable country in Latin America.

"You do understand," I say, "that I can't wear a Diane von Furstenberg wraparound dress in a bird doc."

"I'm shocked that you've even heard of Diane von Furstenberg," he says.

"My mother is in retail."

Then Rigg does something else unexpected. He greets the shopkeeper in Arabic. The man returns the greeting in English. Then, he turns toward the back of the store and a tall, black-eyed beauty with dark hair and exotic eye makeup comes toward us. Next to this voluptuous descendant of Egyptian royalty, I must look like a twelve-year-old boy. If this woman put a bowl of cream on the floor, Rigg would lap it up.

"I am Amaya," she says in a voice as silky as her hair.

"Rigg," Rigg says. "And this is Sophie."

She looks down at me from her greater height. I see her taking in my T-shirt (my mother buys them for me in the men's department of Nordstrom Rack—three for nineteen dollars), the cargo pants, sneakers, and finally, my vest with its many pockets.

"Your sister?" Amaya asks. Her tone is supercilious, as if she can't imagine that a man like Rigg would be with a woman like me.

Rigg shoots me a look and winks. "My wife," he says.

I am surprised by the warmth that spreads from the pit of my stomach toward my chest. Rigg could have joined Amaya in her condescension, but instead, he decided to claim me.

"Ah, she lost her luggage," Amaya says, changing her tune.

"Exactly right. We'll need everything."

When we leave the shop, I am wearing a silk T-shirt, a trench-jacket, cut short like a bolero, a pair of tight black jeans, and sandals with a wedge that raises me up two inches. Without my bulky clothing, I feel unprotected, especially here. Egyptian men are open about their ogling. Rigg, who is holding most of the bags in one hand, slips the other hand through my arm in a proprietary gesture. My usual snippy self would have told him off. After all, I'm a self-sufficient woman, and I don't need a man's protection. But, for once, I keep my mouth shut.

"You look great," Rigg says.

"Thank you."

"We're not finished yet," he adds.

Rigg has paid for everything, claiming that he'd get the money back from Corey West, but I seriously doubt we've been budgeted for this shopping spree. We go into a place called Hair Today, Gone Tomorrow. The sign is in both English and Arabic.

"I've never seen your hair down, not even when you were in the shower," Rigg says. "You always wear a bun."

I wince. "It's not a bun. It's a French twist."

"Well, it looks a lot like a bun, Miss Marple."

I groan. "Now you're comparing me to a nosy English spinster."

"A very clever one," he says.

Inside the salon, Rigg says a few words in Arabic to the squat woman at the front desk, and she leads me to a styling chair. I look at myself. My black glasses are the focal point of my face. I've always loved wearing big glasses. I've been wearing them since high school, even though I don't need them to see and the lenses are clear glass. These glasses are my signature, the way my mother's strings of pearls are hers. She says I've been hiding my light under a bushel. But my real light, the light that matters, has always been about accomplishment and not appearance.

When I take off my specs, I look like a baby bird just coming out of its shell. The stylist takes the combs from my hair and lets it fall over the back of the chair. Both the stylist and Rigg let out a whistle. Besides the occasional trim, my golden-brown hair hasn't been cut since I was eight years old. It cascades below my butt.

"Cut?" the stylist asks, looking at Rigg. The stylist does not exude any of Amaya's sexuality. This woman is named Zan, and her own hair is short on one side and long on the other. I am tempted to ask Zan to refer her questions to me, not to Rigg, but I'm shocked to find out how much I enjoy being Rigg's pretend wife. I like the feeling of him taking care of me, but more than that, I relish in the sense of belonging. It all seems like a dream where I can cut all my hair off now and it will grow back tomorrow.

Rigg stands behind me. I can see both our faces in the mirror. He is handsome. No doubt about that. Chiseled. He snakes his fingers up from my neck to my scalp and fluffs. His fingertips on my skin make me tingle everywhere, even behind my knees.

When hair is as long as mine, with all its weight, it tends to lie flat on top. My part is in the middle. No bangs. No makeup. I am religious when it comes to sunblock and even though I've been outside for the last three days, I look like a ghost. Or maybe a nun. Perhaps a virgin being made ready for sacrifice.

"Take off ten inches," I say. "There will be plenty left. And bangs. I'd like some bangs."

Zan looks at Rigg questioningly. "She means fringe," he says, putting his hand to his own forehead. Then, he rests his hand on my shoulder and looks at me in the mirror. "Are you sure?" he asks.

"Absolutely," I croak. My throat is so dry.

"Could you please get my wife some water?" Rigg asks.

Zan moves off. Rigg pulls up a stool and sits beside me. He takes my hand as if I'm in a hospital about to have a dangerous operation. He doesn't let go when Zan comes back with the water. Rigg continues to hold on as hanks of hair fall onto the shiny tiles.

Chapter 10

RIGG WAS AFRAID that if he let go of Sophie's hand, she'd flip out and change her mind about the haircut. She looked so different after they left the salon. Her hair was long and silky, and she was right to ask for those wispy bangs. She looked less like a penitent about to receive confession and more like a twenty-first-century girl. And she was one hell of a pretty twenty-first-century girl.

Rigg tried to keep his mind off that glimpse of her in the shower. That's when he'd first realized that she might have something to work with. She obviously didn't bother with any landscaping and somehow that made her look more naked, more vulnerable. Most of the girls he'd been seeing, since Nicola asked to take a break, were groomed for a spread in *Hustler.* Pubic hair was a thing of the past. But Rigg wasn't interested in the prepubescent look. A body wasn't more beautiful because of what you managed to remove from it.

Maybe he shouldn't have held Sophie's hand for so long. What did he think he was doing anyway? Part of the reason he was here was to see Nicola. He'd probably already given Sophie the wrong impression.

Sophie was quirky and even charming when she let her guard down. Funny and clever. He wished he was as passionate about something in the way she was about birds. He supposed he was passionate about Nicola. And maybe his yearning to be a director constituted a passion. But directing required a lot of things to come together. Sophie's love of birds didn't demand a crew of people and a big budget. All she needed was her eyes and maybe a pair of binoculars.

Rigg and Sophie walked back toward Starbucks to meet Ahmed. Sophie had a new spring in her step. She was cheerier, more relaxed. She hadn't put her big glasses back on, and Rigg wondered how she was managing to see.

But she obviously could see, because she noticed a commotion that was going on in the direction of the beach.

"Do you know what's happening over there?" Sophie asked Ahmed when they reached him. He was sipping from a very large cup.

"They are filming *Nefertiti*. Nicola Upton is the star. I am very keen on Miss Upton. I think she is the most beautiful of women," Ahmed said. Then he looked at Sophie in surprise. "You are Sophie Castle, yet you are not Sophie Castle," he said.

"I am Sophie Castle." She laughed.

"My heavens, your hair. Very beautiful. Where are your glasses?"

"In my bag," she said.

"Don't you need them?" Ahmed asked.

"Not right now."

"I must say. I am both stunned and astounded."

"Get used to it," Rigg said. "The new Sophie."

"I liked the old one, but this one is very nice, too," Ahmed said.

"Thank you, Ahmed." Sophie's smile lit up the night like a lantern. This was the first time Rigg had seen that smile. It made him feel like he'd just accomplished something wonderful. "Let's go over to the set."

"I agree. We should go over there," Ahmed said.

This wasn't the way Rigg had planned it. He wanted to wait for an opportune moment. He had intended to get cleaned up and present himself at Nicola's hotel. He wanted to romance her, to convince her that it was time for their break to be over. He wasn't going to do that by standing on the edge of Nicola's film set like any ordinary plebe. But Sophie and Ahmed were already headed toward the fracas and there was nothing Rigg could do but follow. Maybe Nicola wouldn't see him.

Years ago, Rigg saw Nicola for the first time at university. She had been playing Cecily in a production of *The Importance of Being Earnest*. Rigg always thought that Nicola's strength was in being both beautiful and funny. She'd taken fewer comic roles lately, and this Egyptian epic certainly wasn't one. This was a big costume extravaganza that was reportedly over budget. His film and Nicola's were chalk and cheese.

Rigg tried to hang back and hide in the crowd, but even from where he was he could see Nicola in her Nefertiti regalia. Her skin was bronzed with a shiny powder. First love is such a powerful thing, especially if you never manage to get over it. Rigg wondered if things would have been different had both of them continued to struggle together in their cramped Venice Beach bungalow. But Nicola got her big break in *Wishes for Fishes*. Then she signed with Coleman Stiffler at CAA and not long after that, she became an "incoming call." That meant that all her agent had to do was sit behind his desk and take offers.

After Rigg learned the term, it became his dream. He wanted to become an incoming call. Not only was he not an incoming call; his current job was a favor to a more flourishing friend. Rigg knew he should take joy in his friends' achievements, but instead, the chip on Rigg's shoulder got heavier and heavier. By the time Nicola told him she wanted to take a break, Rigg felt like the chip had deformed him; he had limped away like the Hunchback of Notre-Dame.

Rigg was thrown out of his trance when he was jostled forward until he was at the edge of the crowd closest to the action. Nicola looked up from a table covered in food. She held a carrot in her mouth like an orange cigarette. When she saw Rigg, she stood absolutely still. Then, she started to float toward him. She was too graceful to walk like an ordinary woman. She drifted, she hovered, she sailed. Though they had lived together for two years, Rigg still found Nicola's beauty otherworldly. It jolted him, raised his temperature, set his heart to pounding. One sight of her turned Rigg into a jellyfish.

"What on earth are you doing here?" Nicola asked. She leaned toward him and kissed him on the lips. It was a soft kiss, but one that was making an offer. Rigg sensed Sophie and Ahmed staring.

When Rigg pulled away, he choked out, "I'm filming a documentary." He drew himself up so that he was standing as straight as he could. At six foot two, he could tower over Nicola and somehow that made him feel better.

"Should I believe that?" Nicola pulled out her flirty voice. Rigg knew the tone well.

Then from behind him, Rigg heard, "It's true. He is filming a documentary on the migratory habits of birds." Sophie edged in beside him.

"So commendable," Nicola said. "Rigg, I always knew you were the best of us." Nicola turned toward Sophie. "Rigg, aren't you going to introduce me to your friend?"

"This is Sophie Castle. She's an ornithologist." Though Rigg had been feeling closer and closer to Sophie all day, when faced with Nicola, Sophie turned back into the nerd scientist he'd been saddled with. Rigg felt a tug on his shirt and turned to the man next to him. "And this is Mr. Ahmed Said. Our translator and driver," Rigg added.

"It is so very brilliant to meet you, Miss Upton. Such a great honor."

"Thank you, Mr. Said." Nicola turned her signature smile on him, the one that could melt an iceberg in less than a minute.

"Oh, call me Ahmed. Please."

Nicola nodded.

"We should be getting back," Sophie said.

"Must you?" Nicola looked at Rigg. "Can't you stay? My driver can take you back to wherever you're going."

"Are you sure?" Rigg asked. "It's almost an hour away."

"Darling, I haven't seen a familiar face in weeks. Besides, I've been missing you."

"You have?"

"So much. Come have dinner with me at my hotel."

Rigg looked over at Sophie, who was digging around in her new handbag. She took out her glasses and put them on.

"Will you two be all right without me?" Rigg asked.

"Of course. Of course," Ahmed said.

"We'll take the bags," Sophie said and held out her hands.

Nicola took Rigg's arm and led him toward her trailer. When he stepped up to the door, he turned from his elevated position to look back toward the crowd, but he couldn't see Sophie. She had disappeared.

Chapter 11

WHEN RIGG LEFT with Nicola, I felt like someone had poured a bucket of ice water on my head. My new clothes might as well be rags, and my coach turned back into a pumpkin. Ahmed and I return to the car and stow the shopping bags in the trunk. Ahmed opens the passenger door and makes a gallant little bow.

We drive out of the city in silence. Ahmed shoots me a worried look.

"That Nicola Upton—she is not so much," he finally says.

"She's only an incredibly beautiful major movie star."

"You, also, are beautiful." He is looking at me, not at the road, and even though he's being kind, his lack of attention to the driving is making me jangly.

"It doesn't matter anyway. I'm not about that external stuff."

"You are lovely no matter what you are about." He pauses. "You should marry me," he says. He is looking straight ahead, through the windshield at the ribbon of macadam in front of us. "I want to go to Hollywood. You are a nice woman. A pretty woman. I will marry you and go to Hollywood."

I bite my lip to keep from laughing. I hardly expected my first marriage proposal to come from a twenty-year-old driver—not that there's anything wrong with being twenty or being a driver, for that matter.

"I want to marry for love," I say.

"This is not always so practical."

Now I can't keep from laughing. Ahmed is serious.

"You Americans think you know about marriage, but you are not so good at it."

"How do you know?"

"American television."

"Don't believe everything you see on TV," I say, thinking that he is probably getting his information from shows like *Scandal* and *The Affair*.

When we get back to the Pigeon House, the sky is an enormous sapphire. Within the hour, the blue will turn to black. I sit on the patio and wait for the stars to come out. When I was little, my mother put the constellations on the ceiling of my bedroom with glow-in-the-dark stickers. It was nothing like this sky. If she had tried to put up this many stars, she'd still be doing it.

Katya comes over and I order pita bread, hummus, and a glass of wine.

"You have hair," Katya says.

"Always did."

"But it was in that terrible bun."

"It was a French twist."

"A distinction without a difference," she says.

"You speak better English than I do."

"I was born in Norway, but I grew up mostly in England. I'm taking a gap year before university." She sits down. "So, Rigg did not come back with you?"

"No."

"You know what they'd call Rigg in England?"

"Full of himself. Rude. Drop-dead gorgeous?"

She laughs. "They'd call him a nob."

"A what?"

"Someone who comes from the upper classes. And then there's knob with a *K* that means the tip of the penis. It's also a person who is a moron or a persistent irritant without even knowing it."

"Rigg fits into both categories."

Ahmed comes through the backdoor to the hotel and sits down with us.

"I have asked Sophie to marry me," he tells Katya.

"You can't ask every American woman you meet to marry you," Katya says.

"And why not? Don't I want to live in America? I want to be in the movies."

"Don't be stupid," Katya says.

"Just because you are my cousin does not mean you can spit on my dreams."

"Don't confuse movie stars with people who really matter. People who do important work—like Sophie," Katya says.

"When I am a star, I will go on television and do a public service announcement," he says. "This way, I reach lots of people, and they will listen to me because I am famous."

Back in my room, I take out my recorder. I need to play something appropriately mournful. The theme from *Love Story* or from Zeffirelli's *Romeo and Juliet* should do the trick. I shouldn't have let myself get carried away today. I remind myself that everything Rigg did, all the attention he gave me, was all in pursuit of a better project.

After fifteen minutes, I have made myself cry. I hear a knock on the door. My heart leaps, and a squawk comes out of the instrument. Maybe Rigg has come to tell me that dinner with Nicola was a bust. I take a look in the mirror, flick a strand of hair off my face, and go to the door.

"If you continue to play those sad songs, I'm going to shoot myself in the head. You'll be responsible for my death," Katya says as she comes in. She is carrying a small case and a large tackle box. I have two similar boxes. One is for fly-fishing (catch and release) and the other holds the watercolors I use to do my bird sketches. Katya puts the case on the bureau and takes out what looks like a very small Crock-Pot. I think she is going to make me some special Middle Eastern beverage, but after she plugs in the tub, and it begins to heat up, I know from the smell that whatever is in there, I'm not going to drink it.

Katya turns and examines my face. "Your brows need some work. They are like an overgrown garden."

"What's in the pot?"

"Wax. I'm going to wax your eyebrows."

"Is it going to hurt?"

"A little. Especially if it's your first time."

"Do you wax your eyebrows?"

"Of course. Brows define the face. Sit here. We'll pretend we are at a spa."

I take a deep breath, sit on the straight wooden chair, and close my eyes. I feel Katya painting warm liquid just above my brow line. It is almost relaxing. Next, she presses something onto the wax and rubs a finger across the spot. So far, so good.

Then, *rrrrip!* She pulls the cloth and the wax from my head. It's worse than tearing off a Band-Aid. Way worse.

"Holy crap."

"It only hurts for a second."

I reach up to my forehead. "Why would anyone in their right mind do this?"

"It's for women who don't want to look like cavemen. Don't touch," she says, but it's too late. There are a few pinpricks of blood on my finger. "I'll put on some cortisone cream," she says. "Look." She holds out a small piece of linen with pink wax stuck to it and embedded in the wax is a caterpillar of tiny hairs. I'm afraid she has taken the entire brow, but when I glance in the mirror, there's plenty left. There's a patch of angry skin on my forehead over my right eye.

I am tempted to ask her to stop, but then I'll be lopsided.

When she is finished, the brows have the shape seen on a 1940s movie star, and it's amazing how submitting to a little pain can improve the appearance. I have to admit that she's created a certain symmetry.

Next, Katya flips open the tackle box on the bureau to reveal shelves of makeup.

"I don't wear makeup. All I wear is sunblock."

"Sunblock is good. You don't want your face to look like an old shoe, but a little color doesn't hurt, especially if you are going to be on camera."

"It's ridiculous for an ornithologist to wear makeup."

"Why?"

"It just is. We are outdoorsy people."

"Let's say you were looking at a beautiful drawing, but the lines were so light that you had to squint to see it."

"And your point?"

"Your eyelashes. They are blond. But long. Add some mascara and you'll be able to see them." She pulls out a tube of something and waves it in front of my face like a wand. Because she is meaning to be kind, I submit to the rest of her ministrations. I don't find it relaxing. I take a deep breath. "Don't sigh like that. It's unattractive," Katya says. After what feels like forever, she says, "You can look now."

When I step to the mirror, I see a face that is both mine and not mine. I am amazed by the results. Nothing doughy. Everything is defined. My eyes, brown with a touch of olive, are now the color of jade. Before Katya leaves, she gives me a lesson in how to apply the makeup myself. Then, she puts a pile of supplies on the bureau.

"I never thought I'd be thanking someone for making me wear makeup. But, thank you, Katya. I think this will look good on film."

"It looks good on *you*," she says.

I glance at the mirror again. Katya has colored me in. It's like I was one of those adult coloring books that are all the rage. And though I'm not usually a fan of coloring between someone else's lines, I can't take issue with this.

Chapter 12

I FIGURE THE chances of Rigg showing up this morning are fifty-fifty. But there he is waiting by the car when I come out wearing the new clothes and cosmetics. It turns out that I'm pretty deft with a makeup brush. It must be all that bird painting.

Rigg gives me an appraising glance.

"You're still wearing the vest," he says.

"It's my signature." I don't mention the glasses—my other signature. How many signatures is one woman allowed to have? Without the vest, I would feel naked. The silky T-shirt shows everything.

"At least you don't look like a bag of rags."

"That just might be the nicest compliment anyone has ever given me," I say as I get into the backseat.

"I didn't mean that the way it sounded." He looks rough this morning. He hasn't shaved and he has dark pockets under his eyes. Even this haggard look doesn't keep the butterflies from zinging around in my chest. I wish Rigg would tell me what he really thinks of my new look—the skin-tight jeans, the nearly transparent T-shirt. And now, the mascara and lip gloss—my newly defined face. I want him to give me that look he gave me yesterday after he saw my hair for the first time. I know I'm being crazy and never thought it was possible for my feelings to change so much in only a day. But though I knew the guy was seductive, now I know he can also be very kind.

Today we are going out to St. Catherine's Monastery, an ancient walled city at the foot of Mount Sinai. It's known for its birds. I thought we could change things up by using a different setting in the documentary. Because this holy site attracts many tourists and pilgrims, we got special permission to get there before the crowd.

We arrive just as the sun is turning pink over the horizon and watch the gorgeous sight from the top of Mount Sinai. Ahmed goes off to wait at a café in the town outside the monastery walls that has grown to serve the tourists.

I want to add the Sinai rosefinch to my life list. So I make it my goal for the day—to see one of these finches. And although that has been a lifelong dream of mine, I'm distracted by thoughts of Rigg and Nicola Upton mixing it up between sheets with an enormous thread count.

Rigg adjusts his tripod.

"How did things go last night?" I can't keep myself from asking.

"It was good to see her," he says.

"When was the last time you were together?"

"About four months ago."

"Then, you aren't exactly a couple."

"I don't really want to talk about it," he says.

"Just making conversation."

Rigg says nothing. He finishes his adjustment, stands up tall, and stretches.

"I didn't say it was good conversation," I say, filling in the gap. "And we don't have to talk about it. But you had a good time?"

"The skies parted and angels started singing." His voice is so deadpan, it almost makes me laugh.

"We should get started."

"Is it true that some birds mate for life?" Rigg suddenly asks.

"Whooping cranes, the mute swan, the bald eagle, the California condor, and a few others."

"The mute swan—that makes sense. Your chances of staying together are better if you can't talk."

"Cynic."

"Have you ever been in a long relationship?"

"What do you mean by *long*?"

"Anything over two years."

"That's so arbitrary."

"Well?"

"There was a guy at Harvard. He was my Nemesis Bird."

"What's that?"

"The bird that eludes you. I tracked the poor guy through every library and bar in Cambridge."

"So, what happened?"

"Eventually, he succumbed to my charms."

"You mean you wore him down." Rigg gives me a roguish smile. I don't know how I feel about being baited at the moment. I'm certainly not about to tell the rest of the story, how after tracking poor Johnson Pinkwater for an entire year, I finally got the nerve to ask him to go for a beer at Grendel's Den. The whole relationship lasted only three months. It took two months for me to realize that Johnson felt the same way about me as he did about fossils; they were mildly captivating, but he was never going to be a paleontologist.

My mother had been philosophical about it. "Honey, you played it all wrong. Men like the chase. They don't want to be hunted."

"That's so sexist, Mom."

"It's biology. Like your birds."

"But what if no one ever picks me?"

She stopped flipping through *Vogue*. "Someone will."

"You're my mother. You have to say that."

She shrugged. "True."

At that moment, an enormous flock of whooping cranes appear from behind the mountain and fill the sky. I look over at Rigg, but he is already filming. Here, where God was supposed to appear to Moses in the form of a burning bush, I am flooded with the feeling that the world is full of wonders, both seen and unseen.

We are engulfed in sound and motion as the cranes move across the horizon. When they are gone, I turn to Rigg.

"You get it now?" I ask.

"Okay, I admit it. That was humbling."

"Looks like there's hope for you yet." That's when I realize he is still filming me, and our conversation is being captured on tape.

"Let's walk," I suggest.

Rigg takes the camera and shoves the rest of the equipment into a backpack. I lift my binoculars. This is a unique birding opportunity, and I don't want to miss a thing.

I see both a white-crowned wheatear and a European bee-eater. I point out what Rigg should film. After ten minutes of silent filming, Rigg stops.

"It's a little static, Sophie. Just birds sitting on branches."

"But can't you see how beautiful they are? How amazing it is that they are here at all? How can I make you understand?"

"Tell me what kind of families they have?" He lifts the camera.

"They're birds. They have bird families."

"The white-crowned wheatear looks like it's wearing a tuxedo," Rigg says.

"And he has a gift for mimicry," I add.

"Good. Keep going."

"They love stony desert environments and cliffs so this is a perfect spot for them. They won't be mating until January or February."

"And what do they do when they're not flirting with each other?"

"They look at us looking at them and wonder what on earth we find so interesting."

"I wonder that sometimes myself," Rigg says.

"They feast on insects," I reply.

"Delicious."

We banter back and forth about the laughing dove, the red-backed shrike, and the spectacled bulbul. It's a great day for seeing birds and finally, when I think I'm going to have to leave without seeing the one bird I came for, two Sinai rosefinches pop up almost beside us. My heart is beating fast as it always does when I add another species to my life list.

I explain how that species goes in my life list and even take out my notebook to show the audience how I log the birds and how this log is the history of my life since I saw my first bushtits in the woods at TreePeople.

"Bushtits?" Rigg asks.

"They're birds," I say. I'm not taking the bait. I'm a scientist for God's sake, not a puerile adolescent.

"Bushtits?" Rigg says again.

"They're tits that hang out in bushes," I explain. This only makes it worse. Rigg begins to laugh.

"I don't see what's so funny," I say, though of course I do; I'm not in a coma.

This makes Rigg laugh even harder until he is doubled over and choking for breath. He walks toward me, drops the camera so it's hanging from his neck, and puts both hands on my shoulders.

"You are one of the funniest girls I've ever met," he gasps.

I decide to take this as a compliment because the feeling of his hands on my shoulders is sending shockwaves through my body. I try to tell myself this is a simple biological response to an extremely attractive man, but really, I think it's more than that. In fact, I know it is.

Chapter 13

IT IS DARK by the time we get back to the Pigeon House. We have been having so much fun; I don't want the day to end.

"Should we get dinner?" I ask.

Rigg smiles and pats me on the shoulder. Even though it's the same kind of pat he might give Ahmed, I feel a flutter. I try to hold it together. If I'm not careful, I might start running around maniacally like a lekking bird.

"I think we deserve a good dinner. You did a great job today, Sophie. Astounding. We'll take a look at the film after we eat something and see what we have. I have a good feeling about it."

"You do?"

"Stop fishing for compliments," Rigg says.

"I wouldn't do that." I look up into his eyes. They are dancing now. I wonder what he looks like when his eyes smolder. It gives me a physical pain in the pit of my stomach when I think that there might have been smoldering eyes last night with Nicola. *So, don't think about it, Sophie. It's not your business anyway. Get out of this fantasy before it's too late. This is not the man for you.*

My body is doing things that my mind would not necessarily tell it to do. My eyes hold Rigg's. I lick my lips. I look over one shoulder as I walk through the bar to choose a table. I think I may be flirting. *Who is this person, and what's happened to Sophie?* I don't care. I'm glad that uptight bitch is gone. She can always come back later.

Rigg pulls out my chair, and since I'm not expecting it, I almost land on the floor. I try to cover my awkwardness and sit down with as much grace as I can muster. He orders a bottle of wine. After my first glass, I start to relax.

I am having a terrible urge to touch Rigg. His face, open now and lacking that tinge of bitterness, is captivating. I want to put my hand on each side of it and look at him until I've had my fill, and with the way I feel at the moment, that might be never. He looks less polished tonight with a scruff of a beard and rumpled khakis. Yet still, he'd never be a misshapen pebble on the beach. He'll always be one of the bright and shiny ones, and against my better judgment, I want to pick up this perfect stone and put it in my pocket.

It's hard to concentrate when someone is having this effect on you. I feel a little demented. I'm like the coyote in the cartoon who looks down to realize he's running in midair. But maybe if he never looked down, he could have kept on going. So I'm not going to look down.

I toss my hair back. A new sensation. Rigg is looking at my lips. A strand of hair falls toward my mouth as I take a bite of spanakopita. I tuck the hair behind my ear.

"You may be the only woman I've ever met who doesn't have pierced ears."

"I'm not into poking holes in myself for decoration," I say, knowing that sounds like the Sophie I am trying to banish. "Do you think I should get my ears pierced?" I add, lifting my chin and putting one finger to my lobe.

"I'd like to see you in earrings that dangle like chandeliers."

"Why?"

"Contrast. They are so feminine."

"Are you saying I'm not feminine?"

"Finish up that enormous plate of food. I want to go look at the dailies."

I follow Rigg to his room. Everything he has used since we arrived has taken up residence somewhere on the floor. I have to be careful not to trip on pants, sneakers, hiking boots, and video equipment.

"I haven't had time to clean up."

"You must have gotten back very late last night."

I want him to say that he came in just after I did. I don't want to think about him spending the night with Nicola.

Rigg turns off the lights and turns on the computer. The videos he took of the ruffs appear on his screen. The birds are truly ridiculous, and that's what I'm saying in the video as I walk toward the camera. I've always given my birds characteristics that go beyond anything that can be observed scientifically. But it's something I always kept to myself.

Rigg has somehow popped open the fun-house door in me. I try not to think about the ornithological community and what they might think of this approach to bird-watching. They aren't the ones with this opportunity, though, and I have to take it and make it my own. I turned the male ruffs into Don Juan and Casanova and the females into twittering spinsters named Henrietta and Doris.

I once saw a man do this with bears. They called him the Grizzly Man, and he got lots of attention. He even made an appearance on *The Late Show with David Letterman*. He wasn't a scientist, and as I watched him getting closer and closer to the bears on video, all I could think was that he was asking for trouble. One October, when he stayed too long at the party, one of his beloved bears ate him for dinner. You can pay a heavy price when you fail to respect the wildness of nature. However, I don't think a flock of birds is going to attack me Hitchcock-style for making up a few stories about them.

When Don Juan flits toward Henrietta on the screen, he causes such a ruckus that Rigg and I laugh hard enough to fall back on the bed, gasping for breath. And then we stop. We are lying beside each other on the bed, looking up at the ceiling. My breathing is ragged. Rigg rolls onto his side and looks at me.

I want him to stay like that forever, and at the same time, I want to hide. It's too much scrutiny, even with just the light from the computer screen.

"And that's what happens when the male is the better-looking one in a species," I say. I don't get up. I don't look toward him.

"You mean he makes himself look idiotic?" Rigg says.

"I don't think that's what I'm saying."

Rigg reaches over, takes my hand, and pulls me up.

"Sit there," he says.

He goes over to the sink, wets a washcloth, and comes back to sit beside me.

"What are you going to do?"

"Wash off that stage makeup." He removes my glasses and puts them on the side table. Then, he rotates the washcloth in gentle circles on my skin. I clench my fists. He might as well be stroking my thighs. He gets to my chin, then my throat. If I had my way, this would go on forever, but he stops and I open my eyes. "Come here." He leads me over to the mirror and turns on a lamp. There is my naked face. "You are beautiful, with or without makeup. You know that, don't you? I want you to know that so when I do this"—He takes my face between his hands and leans in. I close my eyes. At his first kiss, waves of sensation surge through me—"you will know that it isn't the new Sophie who has seduced me. It's the original one."

There is a tiny piece of sanity left in my body. "I think this is probably a bad idea," I choke out. Rigg turns off the lamp. The only light left in the room is coming from the computer where the birds are mating in a continuous loop.

Rigg pulls off my T-shirt. For once, I'm glad I let my mother shop for my underwear. Not that I want to be thinking about my mother at this moment, but she has always had a thing for beautiful underwear, and thanks to her, my delicates are lace confections from France. Even the name of my underwear—Simone Perele—is more romantic than I am. Rigg lets out a gratifying whistle when he sees my demi-cup with its red satin embroidery. I lie back on the bed, and he leans over me.

"My God. Ever since I caught you in the shower, I haven't been able to stop thinking about this spectacular body you've been hiding under all those awful clothes," he says. I begin to unbutton his shirt, but he tears the whole thing off and throws it across the room.

He moves his hand around to my back. He's a master at the one-handed hook release, and a second later, there isn't even a scrap of fabric between my breasts and his chest. He looks into my eyes as if gauging whether to continue. I answer him with a kiss. We scuffle with his jeans and mine. When we are naked, I reach around to touch the back of his head, his neck, his shoulders, elbows, and arms. I could become addicted to this sumptuous feeling of skin upon skin.

"You probably sleep with all your leading ladies," I say. The words pop out like a protective shield.

"My previous leading ladies have been sharks," he mumbles as he gently takes my nipple between his teeth.

I wonder if he means it literally or figuratively, but it doesn't matter. I'm too far gone to turn back. This is once-in-a-lifetime chemistry. Every caress sends a jolt through me.

We make love, and it ends in an orgasm so intense I feel as if I were on a zero-gravity carnival ride, and the centrifugal force is strong enough to throw me back against the spinning wall.

We collapse, limbs akimbo. Rigg wakes me later by softly licking the inside of my thigh, and we begin again, this time looking into each other's eyes.

The last thought I have before falling asleep is that he can't possibly love Nicola Upton if he has this connection with me.

Chapter 14

RIGG DIDN'T PLAN to sleep with Sophie. In fact, the previous night with Nicola had started off better than he could have expected. When he met her at her luxury hotel suite, she let him into her room wearing only her silk dressing gown. That would have told him something once, when he could read the unspoken language of Nicola. He couldn't anymore, and it had surprised him. Maybe it was because in the few days he'd spent with Sophie—that uptight, annoying, impossible, nature-loving vegetarian—the nuances of Nicola became less important. That was hard to believe after all this time, after all the intention he'd put into loving her.

If Nicola had presented herself to him in a robe three days ago, he would have known just what to do. He would have taken her straight to bed, a way of breaking the barrier that had formed between them. They would have been Rigg and Nicola again, and he would have sweet-*nothinged* her back into the relationship.

"Sit down, darling," Nicola had said. She indicated a place

on the love seat, but he chose an armchair. The "darling" didn't mean much. She called everyone darling. That tick had come along at about the time she got her dazzling new teeth.

"Champers?" She got up, went to get a bottle of champagne, and brought it back to him so he could open it.

Sophie would have opened it herself, or at least tried to, if only to show she could. There was no artifice in Sophie.

It shocked Rigg that he was thinking about Sophie when he was with Nicola, his holy grail. During one of their filming sessions, Sophie had fallen over into the swampy land near the beach, and she just picked herself up and brushed herself off as if nothing had happened, even though her bum was wet for the next three hours. Nicola would have acted like she'd been hit by a tsunami and needed to be airlifted out of the park by the Royal Air Force.

Before Rigg met Sophie, he knew exactly what he wanted. Now he found himself popping champagne for a celebration he no longer felt like having.

Nicola perched on the arm of his chair. She smelled of jasmine and roses; it was the expensive perfume she loved—Joy by Jean Patou.

Rigg filled the two delicate champagne flutes that Nicola had set on the low glass table. Then he handed her a glass and took one for himself.

"To us," she said, tilting her glass toward his. They could have been an advert for Perrier-Jouët.

Rigg looked in Nicola's blue eyes. She held them open wide

as if she were constantly on the verge of surprise. At first, Rigg had found this appealing because the expression made him feel as if she were hanging on his every word, but when he found out that it was a technique she learned from her acting teacher, it lost its charm.

"You can't imagine how relieved I was when I saw you standing there with all the other gawkers. It's been a difficult shoot. It takes three hours just to get into makeup. So, what are you really doing here?"

"I'm really doing a documentary on migratory birds."

"That sounds deadly." She moved so that her dressing gown slipped open, showing a sliver of breast. Her skin was so smooth. She used Viktor & Rolf Bonbon Satin body powder she bought at Bergdorf Goodman. Rigg knew this because it used to be one of the things he could buy for her, knowing she wouldn't be disappointed with it.

"Actually, it's turning out better than I could have expected," he said.

"You did know I'd be here, didn't you?" She kissed his cheek, snaking her tongue up toward his earlobe.

"I knew," he admitted.

She took his hand, the one not holding the champagne glass, and put it on her breast. She'd always felt like home to him, since the first moment he met her at university, but something was off. Her breast didn't feel familiar. It was much firmer than it had been, almost rock hard.

"I had them done," she said. She slipped her robe from her

shoulders, revealing two perfect perky breasts. "How do you like them?"

"What was wrong with the old ones?"

"I wanted the nipples to be a bit higher and to give my breasts more volume. What do you think?"

He touched each one unwillingly. They were unyielding. "Where are the scars?"

"That's the beauty of it. You can barely see them. I don't mind doing full-frontal nudity now. It's like my tits aren't really mine anymore. They're someone else's work of art. And they'll soften up. It will just take time. When I saw you standing there on the edge of the beach, that was the first thing I thought. *Wait until he sees these.*" She held each breast in her hand as if she were modeling for a skanky magazine. It wasn't as if Rigg had never seen fake breasts before. After all, he had been living in Los Angeles for six years. Still, he was jarred by these. He had been very satisfied with Nicola's breasts the way they were before. Rigg poured some more champagne.

"I wish we could have discussed it," he said.

"But we weren't together," she said.

"Exactly." He stood up. "I should get going. I have to be up with the sun."

"I thought you'd stay," she said.

"Nicola, I don't want to jump into bed. We have things to discuss first."

"Like what?"

"Like whether you just want to have sex or whether you want to get back together."

"Does it matter?" she asked.

"Of course it does."

"It's just sex," she said.

"Not to me. Not with you."

And then came the next day and something he never expected to happen did. He slept with Sophie. When he woke up, she wasn't in bed. He found her in the restaurant where she was eating a mountain of toast, avocados, and tomatoes.

"Good morning," she said. "You should order breakfast before they stop serving."

He moved to kiss her, but she leaned away and looked around. "Don't."

"Why not?"

"It's unprofessional."

"Who's going to see us?"

"Ahmed."

"And what difference would that make?"

She didn't have a good answer for that. Rigg ordered breakfast, and they sat across from each other.

"We'll focus on the birds at sunset tonight since we're getting such a late start," Sophie said.

"I think everyone should spend at least one day a week naked," Rigg said.

Sophie looked up and laughed.

"You're a little off subject, aren't you?"

"Am I? Maybe we should go back to my room and play Garden of Eden."

Rigg poked his fork into a slice of apple from his fruit plate and fed it to Sophie. "Stop acting like nothing happened last night," Rigg said.

Sophie put down her toast and bit her bottom lip. "I don't want it to get in the way of the work. We have only one more day to make something great."

"I thought last night was pretty great," Rigg said.

Sophie wiped her lips with a napkin. "It was just sex. We should get going or we'll lose the whole day." She stood up, but Rigg held her by the forearm.

"Sit down," he said in a low voice. She sat. "It was not just sex. I like you. Your quirky independence, your silly recorder, those ridiculous glasses that you don't really need, your devotion to the birds, and, to be honest, even that stupid safari vest is beginning to grow on me. You make me see things I didn't want to see about myself.

"I've been given everything; the best education money could buy. Good friends. Even work I like. But all I could think about is how I didn't have the success that my friends had. Somehow, that turned into arrogance—God only knows how. I've been abrasive and self-centered. No wonder everything blew up in my face."

Sophie sat down, reached over, and took his hand. "You're not that bad." With her other hand, she picked up her fork, reached over to his plate, stabbed a slice of apple, and put it in her mouth.

Chapter 15

RIGG WAS SWEET at breakfast, and I acted like a prat. That's a word he'd use. *Prat*. He tells me that what happened between us wasn't just sex. Don't I know it. It was mind blowing. Life altering. The problem is that elation and fear are duking it out in my chest, and though I'm rooting for elation to win—standing in its corner with a bottle of water and a towel—fear is one big bruiser. What if, what if, what if…

On our way out to Wadi Khoshbi in the park, I make some notes. I can't plan as much as I'd like to. So much depends on the birds. At the bottom of my list, I make a small *ML*. It stands for "made love," but if anyone asks, I can say it means "migrating lapwing."

It's already hot by the time we unload the equipment. That's one of the reasons we've done most of our work first thing in the morning. Ahmed brought a sun canopy, something we haven't needed so far, but today we are not near the sea and there is no shelter from the pounding sun. My old clothes, the ones we replaced, were made by a company that specializes in fabric that protects you from UV rays, but the more glamorous outfit I'm wearing now is screaming, "Give me skin cancer."

Ahmed agrees to come back and get us at dusk.

When I see both a red-backed shrike and a yellow-vented bulbul in one hour, Rigg is able to catch my excitement on video. I name the birds Mike and Fred and tell a story about how they meet here every year to play golf. I briefly wonder what my ornithologist colleagues will think of this. But I don't care that much. They aren't the ones who have a deal with the Discovery Channel.

"Rigg, do you think this looks stupid?" I ask.

He puts his arm around me and pulls me close. "It's entertaining. It's funny. It's not stupid." He gives me a kiss, all-encompassing and tasty. It makes me so wobbly that I have absolutely no idea whether he's telling me the truth, and I don't care. There is not another person for miles and miles, at least that's what it feels like. Rigg pulls at the snaps of my vest. His hands slide inside my shirt. I reach for him. I can't get enough of the feel of him—his smooth chest, flat stomach, strong hips.

"We shouldn't be doing this," I say.

"Maybe not." He takes my hand and leads me over to a dune. He takes a pouch from his pocket and when he opens it, a full-sized blanket floats out like Aladdin's flying carpet.

We scramble out of our clothes. I feel both panic and exhilaration. If, on that first day, when I saw Rigg relaxing in the bar after he'd left me at the airport because he hadn't felt like waiting, someone had told me I'd be head over heels in love with the guy, I would have had them committed. I'd have said that I could never, no matter how good-looking he was, fall in love with a man who was so arrogant, so snide, so seriously in need of an attitude adjustment.

But his lips on my nipple don't feel arrogant. To be naked out there under the sun is a freeing sensation. Even my toes are zinging with the high-voltage crackle of love. And just as we are beginning to believe that we are the only people on earth, we hear a motor.

We jerk up. An open tour bus is coming in our direction. This is the only time we've ventured inland and we must be near a particularly compelling spot, because this is the first time we've been confronted with a gaggle of tourists.

"Damn," Rigg says. "If we don't do something fast, we're going to end up as this tour's main attraction." He grabs me and, locked in an embrace, we roll down the dune and into a crevasse. Rigg pulls the blanket over us, and now we're in a cave of our own making. The idea of having sex right there where we could be so easily caught is more stimulating than I could ever have imagined.

I have definitely lost my mind. We can hear the voice of the tour guide over the loudspeaker. The bus has stopped, but the two of us haven't.

"What if they get out and start looking around?" I whisper into Rigg's chest.

"They'll see the mating ritual of the great *Homo sapiens*," he murmurs back.

I giggle. "We've got nothing on the ruffs."

"We do okay." Rigg kisses my neck. His fingers are exploring nooks in my body that I hardly knew existed. "You ever wonder if they enjoy it?"

"If who enjoy what?" I am gasping for air and trying to keep as quiet as I can.

"If the birds enjoy mating as much as humans do, or if it's simply a biological imperative." He slides his tongue into my belly button.

"If the birds get even half the pleasure you're giving me, we don't have to worry about them." The feel of Rigg's chest against mine is all I can concentrate on.

"Sophie, love, you give scientific exploration new meaning." He sinks his fingers into my hair. And that's when we stop talking.

Chapter 16

FOR ONCE IN my life, I've found something more alluring than the birds. We stay in our hiding place until the sound of the tour bus's engine disappears. We giggle between kisses. I wonder if anyone has heard us. I picture a mother explaining it to her kid. *That, Henry dear, is the sound of pure joy.*

I have absolutely no interest in looking at birds, perhaps for the first time since I was eight. We probably have enough footage right now, but we might as well get all we can. I push myself up and start to pull on my jeans and T-shirt. I'm hoping we get one more shot of a big stork migration. The script I have prepared for today is about the instinct to fly halfway across the world to find hospitable weather. Maybe I can equate it with old people going to Arizona for the winter.

"Oh, shit," Rigg yells.

I turn around. Rigg is holding his thigh and rocking back and forth. He begins to repeat, "Oh, shit," over and over again like a mantra. "I've been bitten."

"Come on. Stop kidding around. We should get back to work."

"I'm serious. I think it was a cobra."

I walk over to him and take a look at his leg. "You'll need to get dressed." I keep my voice calm.

"I'm not sure I can."

"I'll help you." I lean down for his boxer briefs and slide them over his feet. He is beginning to sweat.

"I don't feel well," he says.

"Did you see the snake?" I ask, keeping my voice casual.

"I swear it was sizzling in the heat."

A carpet viper. My pulse speeds up. There aren't too many things that can happen in the wild to freak me out, but this is one of them. All you can do for this kind of snakebite is get the victim to the hospital as soon as possible.

"Poisonous?" Rigg asks.

I suck air through my teeth. "Well, yes, a bit."

"A bit?"

"Come on. We have to get out of here."

"How the hell are we going to do that? Oh, shit. Oh, shit. Oh, shit. Suck on it."

"What?"

"The venom. Suck it out."

"You're not supposed to do that."

"Then why does everyone think you are?"

"I don't know. It looks heroic."

"Soph, this really hurts."

I kneel down and look at the puncture wounds.

"Tourniquet?" he asks.

"Only if you want your leg to fall off." The wound is beginning to swell. "I know you aren't supposed to cut off the blood supply to the limb."

"What are we supposed to do then?"

"We've got to get you to a hospital." I check my cell phone. Of course, there is no reception out here.

"My legs feel like jelly," Rigg says. He lies flat on his back. With one great groan, he lifts himself up and pulls his Calvin Klein briefs to his waist.

I quickly clean the wound with antiseptic from the first-aid kit in the bottom left pocket of my vest. I don't know how we're going to explain this. Most people get bitten on the ankle.

One of the symptoms after a snakebite is panic. I think Rigg is feeling too ill to panic. Not me. The important thing is for Rigg not to know that I'm freaking out. I have so much adrenaline running through me, I feel like I could lift Rigg in my arms and fly off with him like Supergirl. *If only.*

Pulling a marker from another pocket, I use it to circle the swollen area around the original wound. If I do this every fifteen minutes, it will let the doctors see how fast the venom is spreading.

I wonder how often the tour buses go by—once a day, twice, maybe three times. Ahmed isn't scheduled to come back for hours.

"Don't you have some magic potion in that vest? Antivenom or something?"

"It's actually antivenin." I begin to spell it out.

"Really?" he says. "You actually think this is a teachable moment?"

"Sorry," I say. Rigg has managed to wriggle into his pants at this point. "I'm going to cut off the legs of your trousers, so I can monitor the wound."

"They're expensive."

"So?"

"You really have to ruin them?"

I slip my hand into an interior vest pocket and pull out my Traveler's Army Knife. It has everything from tweezers to a barometer. All I want right now is a pair of scissors. I take Rigg's slacks and start cutting.

"You should have bought zip-off," I say.

"I don't even know what that is."

"They're pants where the legs zip off so they can be used as shorts."

"They sound hideous," he says.

"They may not make a fashion statement, but they would be very useful in this situation." I draw another circle around the wound. The infected area is spreading fast.

Once Rigg has the rest of his clothes back on, he gets up unsteadily. I've done a terrible job with his pants. He looks like a lopsided version of Huckleberry Finn and his boxer briefs show under the shorter leg. But none of that matters. I can see the bite and monitor the infection. Rigg winces as he stands. "Put your arm around my shoulder and lean on me. We're heading toward the entrance of the park," I say.

"How do you know where that is?"

I fish my compass out of my vest pocket—upper right. "It's north."

"I'm never going to make fun of you again."

"That a promise?"

"What about our stuff?"

"We'll have to leave it." I try not to show how much I hate that idea. Anyone could come along and take all our equipment. That could certainly put a monkey wrench into this project. I shove a couple of Rigg's cameras into our emergency rucksack and hoist it onto my back. It's full of water, protein bars, and sunblock. We begin to walk north across an empty plain of dry stone. It's unusually hot for November. To sweat in this heat is normal, but Rigg's clamminess has an unhealthy quality. I know he has a fever, and a part of me is glad I don't have a thermometer because if I found out how high his temperature is, I'd flip. As it is, my attitude is all an act. I'm terrified inside, but outside, I am a rock. I pray that another tour bus will come by. When we didn't need it and certainly didn't want it, one appeared out of nowhere, and now that we're desperate, there isn't a living thing in sight, not even a goddamn bird.

Rigg's top-of-the-line Bimini cap isn't keeping him cool. Nothing will. His heat is coming from the inside. Rigg's arm on my shoulder gets heavier and heavier and just when I'm afraid he's done in, I hear the distinctive rumble of the open tour bus.

I flag it down. At first, it looks like the bus isn't going to stop. I run in front of it and wave my arms. The driver stops and jumps from his seat. He says something in Arabic, and I stare at him.

"You crazy woman?" he says in English. "This is no hop-on, hop-off. This is not the big city."

By now, Rigg is slumping toward the ground. He's close to passing out. One of the passengers, a potbellied man dressed in mushroom-colored safari clothes, comes down the stairs. He puts his hands on his hips and yells at the driver. "Can't you see this man is sick?" The safari-clad man has an English accent and reminds me of a colonel you might find in an Agatha Christie novel. To my shock, he bends down, hoists Rigg over his shoulder in a fireman's lift, and carries him onto the vehicle. Then he lays him down on a padded bench. I follow them.

"George Ashby," the man introduces himself. "My wife, Margaret."

Margaret is dressed like George—mushroom from head to foot.

"Here, dear. Slip in and put his head on your lap. He'll be more comfortable," Mrs. Ashby says.

I nod and make another circle around the swollen area. I stroke Rigg's forehead. His eyes are fluttering and he can't keep them open. Mrs. Ashby leans over the seat and rests a hand on my shoulder. I hear Mr. Ashby's voice coming from the front of the bus. "I'll take full responsibility. Head toward the gate and do it fast. And radio ahead for an ambulance."

I glance at Rigg's thigh. The venom is spreading.

Chapter 17

"MOST SNAKEBITES ARE on the ankle," says Dr. Samara, in the emergency room.

"The snake must have climbed up his pant leg," I say.

"Very bad luck," the doctor says to Rigg. "But at least you had this young woman to help. She did all the right things. If I were you, I'd keep her."

Rigg reaches for my hand. "I just might," he says.

"I think you've overmedicated him, Doctor," I say.

"She's cute," Dr. Samara says.

"She's my own personal Girl Guide," Rigg says.

Dr. Samara takes Rigg's pulse. "We have administered the antivenin. We will put you in a room overnight to make sure the toxin clears your system."

I follow as an orderly rolls Rigg's gurney down the hall. Rigg's room is a double, but there is no one in the other bed. Rigg is groggy, but he reaches out for me. He wants me to lie down beside him, but I feel a little weird about that. I sit on the edge of the bed. Just when I think he is asleep, he opens his eyes and says, "You know, just because you saved my life doesn't mean you are responsible for me."

"I don't mind," I say in a soft voice, but I feel like he's gut-punched me. He has said the opposite of the romantic thing. The right thing would be to say that now I *am* responsible for him, that we are bound together. That's what he'd say if this were *Romancing the Stone,* one of my favorite movies of all time. Then again, maybe he wouldn't say the right thing. It was the woman, Joan Wilder, who said the really romantic stuff. *You're the best time I've ever had.*

"I should probably get going," I say. "Let you get some sleep." I'm afraid Rigg's regretting everything that's happened between us. Rigg and I were in a dream, and the viper woke him.

My hand is still lying on the bed, and I want Rigg to grab my wrist and pull me toward him, but he shuts his eyes as if he'd like to shut out everything, even me.

"Do you want me to tell Nicola that you're here in the hospital?" I ask. The question is against my best interest, but I can't keep myself from asking; I need to know where we stand.

He smiles. "I'll tell her. There's something I need to say to her. Nothing like a near-death experience to put things in perspective." He licks his dry lips.

"You weren't going to die." I give him the cup of water next to the bed.

"Not if you had anything to do with it." His face lights up with the smile I once thought was arrogant.

I get up and when he reaches toward me, I don't move. He

drops his hand back onto the bed. I can't tolerate the idea of him seeing Nicola. If I weren't so afraid of what I might hear, I'd ask him why.

"Sophie, what's wrong?"

"Nothing." I shake my head. I can't look at him.

I've swallowed the words *I love you,* and they are choking me.

Chapter 18

I WOULD HAVE stayed all night at the hospital if Rigg had asked me to, but he didn't. Ahmed is in the waiting area when I come out.

"He's going to be fine," I say.

"I should have stayed with you at the park."

"You gave us the canopy."

"And that did no good."

"We didn't get sunburned," I say. He cracks a smile, a small one. "Let's go home. I want to get drunk."

I sit in the front seat beside Ahmed, and he looks straight ahead. He doesn't talk about marrying me and moving to America.

"You are not responsible for this," I say.

"I went out and retrieved all the equipment. It was all there. Everything. I put it in your room."

"Thank you, Ahmed."

I take a deep breath of relief. Of course, a person is more important than a bunch of stuff, but that stuff is key to this documentary, and I'm glad no one ran off with it.

* * *

In the bar, I order an arak. "Make it a double," I say in the tradition of all spurned lovers everywhere. When Katya brings over the glass, it's a single. "I hate this stuff," I say and drink it all down in a gulp. "Let's have another."

"You want me to have one, too?" Katya asks.

"I'm not stopping you."

"I may be stopping you," she says.

"What do you mean? I've only had one drink, and I have a mission."

Katya puts another glass on the table.

"And what would that be?"

"To blank out this whole day."

"All of it?"

I think of making love in that crevasse with the blanket sheltering us. "Most of it."

"I thought you and Rigg were finally getting along."

"We were." I drink the second drink with gusto even though I hate the stuff. But it's strong and that's all that matters.

"Why don't you go back to your room and play that instrument of yours?"

"It's called a treble recorder. And I don't want to be alone."

"Then bring it out here. You can charm the snakes."

"I don't play in public."

Katya looks around at the smattering of customers. "I wouldn't call this *public*."

"Rigg is going to see his old girlfriend, Nicola Upton. They have history together. He's loved her for ages. And she's a movie star, which, for some reason, makes it much worse. What am I going to do?"

"Nothing," Katya says.

"That doesn't sound like such a great plan."

"You came here looking for birds, not for happily ever after."

"Right, maybe this is just a fling. Maybe he was just being nice to me for the sake of the project and it got out of hand. Do you think I should tell him how I feel?"

Katya slams her hand down on the table. The glasses shake. "When you came here you were sensible and in control. You knew just what you were doing and where you were going. And now look at you! You're a whining piece of apple crumble. You obviously haven't learned *the lesson*." Katya puts air quotes around *the lesson*.

"Is that like *The Secret,* because I'm not sure I believe in all that Law of Attraction stuff."

"*The lesson* is that men are not complicated. If a man wants you, there is never a shadow of a doubt about it. It's simple. Women come up with all kinds of fancy reasons why a man might be acting the way he is: He's shy. He's afraid to ruin the friendship. He's afraid of commitment."

"We never had a friendship to ruin," I say.

"That's not the point. Even if all these things were true, what you'd be getting is a shy, ambivalent man who is afraid of commitment. How very appealing."

I've been so flooded with lust, I haven't been able to think straight. I picture the tide ebbing and take a deep breath of desert air.

"You should go to bed," Katya says. "Things will look different in the morning."

"Why do people always say that? Maybe they'll look worse."

"Come on. I'll give you a to-go cup. You've had a long day."

Back in my room, I take a sip of what's in the cup. I can tell from the smell that it isn't arak. It's the house white. I know because I've downed the stuff before. It tastes a little weird since there's a licorice taste in my mouth, but I like the wine a lot better. I'm not tempted to throw it back.

Our equipment is piled in the corner, and I organize it. I still can't believe it's all here. That's something to be grateful for.

I turn on the computer and look at what we've got. When I see a pattern developing, I edit some pieces together. We may not have a story exactly, but there is a shape, some kind of narrative. There is more footage on mating than on migration, so I use the migration as a frame for a love story. It never occurred to me to wonder if these birds, especially the ones that mate for life, love each other. As a scientist, I'd have to say no, that the connection is mere biology. I suppose I could prove it if I studied it long enough, but I can't imagine that proving the absence of love is a worthy life pursuit. Still, if I could find the secret behind monogamy in certain species, maybe I could apply it elsewhere. Imagine discovering a root cause of faithfulness. Nobel Prize, here I come.

After a few hours, I have put together something I can show to Corey West at Discovery. I could wait for Rigg. I should wait. But this is my project, and Rigg has already made major changes that I never anticipated. It's time to see if we're on the right track.

I upload the file and press Send.

Chapter 19

WHEN RIGG LEFT the hospital the next morning, his thigh still ached. He was surprised that Sophie hadn't come with Ahmed to retrieve him, but it was better this way because he wanted to see Nicola. He called her to find out where she'd be that day. The crew was out at St. Catherine's.

"Do you mind taking me, Ahmed?"

"Wherever you need to go is fine by me."

Rigg thought Ahmed would be more enthusiastic about seeing the film people again, but Ahmed was subdued.

As they drove, Rigg thought about how grateful he was for Sophie's outdoor expertise and even for the stupid vest with its many mysteries. The item of clothing that Rigg had found so ridiculous had offered exactly what they needed like a magical garment in a children's book. He had to admit it; sometimes function was more important than form.

He thought of calling Sophie, but he wasn't sure what he wanted to say to her. One woman at a time. First, he'd deal with Nicola.

When they approached the monastery, the sight that greeted them was far different from the one they'd seen when filming a few days before. With Sophie, they had arrived early in the morning, when all was quiet, even spiritual. Today, the place was swarming with actors and crew.

Nicola looked like she had descended straight from the sun and still had pieces of it glowing from within her. Rigg stood and watched. She seemed very far away, as if she were already a picture on a screen and no longer flesh and blood.

Rigg thought back to the first time they had made love, which had been in his room at university. It was a first for both of them. They were like two puzzle pieces that someone found under the carpet and put back in place. For once, everything felt right. Rigg knew he'd marry this exquisite girl, that they'd scale the heights of fame and fortune together.

It had taken a few years before it all went wrong. And it started with Nicola rocketing to fame, when being Nicola's "plus one" at exclusive events began to be how Rigg was defined in Hollywood.

When they broke for lunch, Nicola waved to Rigg. She slipped off her enormous headdress and came down the steps toward him. Even when she was on his level, she looked too perfect to be human. It was hot, but Nicola didn't sweat. Maybe it was the makeup. She was brushed with gold powder.

Nicola kissed Rigg on the lips, snaking her hands around to the back of his neck. Her mouth always tasted of sugared almonds and Rigg wondered why, because Nicola didn't eat sugar—ever. She was strict about never eating anything white—no flour, no potatoes, no pasta.

"What on earth has happened to your trousers? You look like a country bumpkin," she said when Rigg finally pulled away. "And why are you here? I thought you were doing that bird thing."

She snapped her fingers, and a boy with half his head shaved appeared with a bottle of water.

"I got bitten by a viper yesterday and I've been in the hospital. Sophie cut the legs off my trousers so she could monitor the wound."

"Well, she's no tailor, that's for sure. Why didn't you call me? I would have come."

"I was fine, thanks to Sophie."

"What a useful little person she must be." Nicola upended her water into her mouth and drank like she was dying of thirst.

"Can we go sit down somewhere?" Rigg asked.

"Sure. Come into my trailer."

Rigg followed Nicola to a moderately sized Airstream. Inside, clothes were dripping from every piece of furniture. Rigg and Nicola had the same haphazard approach to housekeeping.

"Sorry. They were supposed to pick up in here," Nicola said. "You want something to drink?"

Rigg shook his head. "I probably shouldn't. I'm not 100 percent. Here, sit beside me."

She snuggled up to him on the banquette and put her hand on his thigh. He winced. "That's where I got bitten."

"Your upper thigh?"

He nodded.

"That's very odd. Most people get bitten on an ankle."

Rigg turned toward Nicola. "Nic, I came to apologize."

"What for?" Nicola looked away. Rigg wasn't sure if she did this for effect or if she was really worried he was going to say something she didn't want to hear.

"I've been an unmitigated ass. I made things so difficult for you with my ego and my resentments. I was never happy for you, the way I should have been. All I could think about was myself and what I wasn't getting, how you and Simon and Philip were becoming huge successes and I was lagging behind."

"Would that be envy or jealousy? I always get them confused," Nicola said, sucking at the inside of her cheek.

"Envy, I think. Nothing to be proud of, in any case."

Nicola put her hands on Rigg's upper arms and looked into his eyes. "I forgive you. There. It's done."

"But I don't want to be forgiven."

"You don't?" She removed her hands. "Then, what is it you want?"

"I want to start all over. Put that horrible Rigg behind me. I've been my own worst enemy."

"I tried to tell you that, but it seems this Sophie girl has had more of an impact on you in one week than I've had in years."

"The thing is, there are these birds I've been filming. In many species, the ruff, for instance, one gender is more decorative. One has all the bluster, and the other is more laid-back, not so colorful, maybe even a little dull. It's called *sexual dimorphism*. In the case of the ruff, the male is the loud one. He is, without a doubt, one of the most ridiculous, self-important, vain birds in the entire animal kingdom. He needs to be the center of attention. That's us, Nic. You and I. We're both male ruffs."

"I think that venom got into your head. Are you saying you want me to be a dull bird? Because that isn't going to happen."

Rigg took her hand. "Of course not. Maybe a part of me wished it, but that's not who you are. In the world of birds, you are a flamingo. You'll never be a sparrow, and I shouldn't want you to be one. You see what I'm saying?"

"I think you might be saying that you don't love me." She removed her hand from his.

"I'll always love you."

"But you don't want to get back together."

He shook his head. "Not anymore."

"I thought that was why you came to Egypt."

"So did I," he said.

"That bird girl seems to have had quite an influence on you. That bitter resentment you've been hauling around like a box of rocks is gone. It was highly unattractive, by the way."

"I suspected as much," Rigg said.

"Did you?" Nicola stood up. Rigg saw past all the glitter to the girl he first fell in love with ten years ago. "I do wish you had figured it out sooner," she said.

Chapter 20

RIGG HOPPED INTO the car. "Let's go home, Ahmed." Rigg's mind felt clearer than it had in years. He couldn't wait to see Sophie. When he stepped into the lobby of the Pigeon House, he could hear the plaintive tune of "Moon River" coming down the hall from Sophie's room. Didn't that girl know any happy songs?

And what did she have to feel so tragic about? Her project was going to be a success. Rigg could feel it. He'd been doing this long enough to know.

He rapped enthusiastically on Sophie's door, but it took a few minutes for her to answer. She looked like she'd been battling a tornado and lost. She was wearing those terrible cargo pants and a T-shirt three sizes too big for her.

"How do you feel?" she asked without meeting his eyes.

"My leg hurts, but I thought you could kiss it and make it better."

Sophie stepped back. "Didn't Nicola take care of that?"

"Of course not. That's your spot. You marked it with a Sharpie."

"I wasn't claiming my territory. I was making sure the infection didn't spread."

"But I want you to claim it."

He walked in and sat on the bed. She turned toward him.

"You do?"

"What did you think this was all about?" he said, opening his arms to her.

"Convincing me to do a better film so you could move up the ladder and get back with your movie star girlfriend?"

"Soph, you've got it all wrong. Come over here."

She walked slowly toward him. When she was a foot from the bed, he reached out and pulled her down to his lap. He ran his fingers through her thick mass of hair, took chunks of it in his fists, and kissed her deeply. When he was a child, his family had a house in the country. Rigg would go on walks with his father, and his father would identify the plants. Once, he reached down and picked some green leaves.

"Chew," Rigg's father had said. Rigg put the leaves in his mouth. "That's wild mint."

Sophie tasted just like that. She pulled away. "But you came here, to Egypt, because of Nicola, didn't you?"

"Partly."

"Well, then, what's changed?"

"Don't you know?"

She shook her head.

"I've fallen in love with you."

She wrapped her arms around Rigg, and they kissed. As far as she was concerned, this kissing could go on for hours, for days, for weeks. It is as if Rigg pours a balm over her burns whenever he kisses her.

Sophie slipped out of her shirt. She wanted to feel Rigg against her. He is still wearing the pants that she cut. She kissed the bite, making circles around it with her tongue. Rigg lies back and moans softly.

"Does it hurt?" she asked.

"Quite the opposite."

She slipped her fingers up until she's cupping him underneath his shorts. This time, he groans and sits up. He pulls off his pants and his boxer briefs. He reaches for the snap on her pants and their fingers fumble together. Finally, they are both naked and holding each other, fused as tightly as they can be. If Sophie could disappear inside that man right now, she would.

They fall onto the bed, facing each other, and for a moment they stop and look into each other's eyes as if trying to fathom what has happened to them. Sophie feels like there has been a cosmic shift in the universe.

Rigg kisses one breast, then the other. His tongue makes its way up to her throat and down to the curve of her belly and beyond.

Each time they are together like this, it gets better. Sophie is learning his body, each freckle and indentation. She's never experienced this: sex and love together. What a leap it is. Like jumping into the Grand Canyon and praying your parachute will open. It is the closest Sophie has ever come to flying.

She's so keyed up, she knows she won't be able to sleep. Her limbs and Rigg's are all braided together. She takes a deep, satisfied breath and closes her eyes. And when she opens them again, it is morning. She reaches over for Rigg, but he's gone.

Chapter 21

WHEN RIGG WOKE at dawn, he turned to look at Sophie. He had been tempted to push back the curtain of her hair so he could see her face, but he didn't want to wake her. He slipped out of bed. He had to think, and he couldn't do it when Sophie was so near. He couldn't be rational around her, not anymore. Even when he was with Nicola last night, he'd been thinking of Sophie. This bird nerd had bewitched him and thrown all of his plans off course.

Last night with Nicola had been something of a revelation. Rigg had loved Nicola for over ten years. Even when they were apart, he kept an eventual life with her as a vision he held before him like a torch to show him the way out of darkness. And now Sophie had come along and turned on all the lights, and the torch was useless.

As soon as Nicola seemed to understand that there had been a seismic shift in Rigg, she stopped flirting with him and pulled out the nostalgia card.

"Remember," she had said, sitting on the sofa with her legs

curled beneath her, "when everything was new? We were so good at being hopeful, the four of us. We believed in ourselves so strongly."

They had all known that sometime in the not too distant future, the Hollywood community would embrace them. And it did—each one in turn: first Simon, then Nicola, and then Philip. But Rigg remained on the fringes, and never got what he wanted. He had viewed the bird documentary as a step down. Even though it was work, and it paid the bills, he saw himself as a failure. The scent of *L'Eau de Underachiever* wasn't attracting the kind of attention he wanted.

"Churchill said that success is stumbling from failure to failure without loss of enthusiasm," Nicola said. "Of the four of us, you're the only one who's made a meal of rejection."

"It's been taking me much longer than you three to get where I want to go."

"I always believed you could get there. We all did."

He might have accused them of letting him flounder, but then he remembered that the Discovery job was courtesy of Philip. How many other opportunities had his friends provided for him that he wasn't even aware of?

"You have to admit that your success came early," Rigg said.

"There were failures. Remember my Lady Macbeth at that little theater on Santa Monica Boulevard? I was atrocious and the reviews were so unkind—'Out, out damned actress.' Even so, I didn't quit. I went on every night, even though I knew I was bad. Philip coached me until I wasn't quite so ridiculous, and I have never done Shakespeare since. I'm not proud of that. Still, that was where my first agent saw me. We never know when or how our big break is going to come." She leaned forward, and Rigg caught a glimpse of the valley between her new breasts. He looked away. She got up and poured him a glass of champagne.

"I told you that won't mix well with my medication," he said.

"What's the worst that could happen?" She sat close beside him. "Let's toast."

"To what?"

"To *Knees Up*."

"What's that?"

"It's Simon's new comedy."

"He didn't tell me about it."

"We had a director and we thought you might be hurt that we didn't ask you, so we didn't tell you."

"You and Simon have done a lot of movies, and I haven't been involved in any of them. I wouldn't have made a big deal of it."

"But we're doing this one together. Philip is doing it, too."

"So, I am odd man out."

"We were afraid you would think of it that way. And when Ben Wheatley agreed to do it, we just had to have him, but now he's fallen out. Seeing you again, I've noticed this change in you. I mean, the old Rigg would have been railing by now. He would have been yelling that he didn't need to be anyone's last-minute replacement. I have never known anyone so good at shooting himself in the foot."

"Are you sure you want me for this? All I have is those comedy shorts I did at university."

"But all of us were in them. And we had so much fun. We thought maybe we could try working together again."

"You'd be taking a big chance on me," Rigg said.

"Wow. Who are you and what have you done with the real Rigg Greensman?"

"Maybe I'm just a little more realistic now."

"Well, it looks incredibly good on you." Nicola went into the bedroom and came out holding a script. "I'm sure you're going to like it."

Rigg took the script, stood up, and headed toward the door. Nicola followed so that when he turned to say good-bye, she was standing so close to him, he could smell the flowery scent of her shampoo.

"Thanks for this. I really appreciate it," he said.

"There's only one catch."

"What's that?"

"You have to leave for Melbourne tomorrow."

"Before Christmas?"

"We are all planning to have Christmas together in Australia."

"Christmas with my three best friends. Wow."

"It's a small independent film, but if it's a success, it will launch you." She leaned over to kiss him, pulling him toward her and wrapping her arms around his neck. He extricated himself gently, lifting off one slender arm and then the other. He smiled down into the face he had loved for so long. "Simon is already there with some of the crew. I just have to finish up here. We'll have a great time, the four of us together again."

"I'll read the script," he said, but he already knew he was going to do the film. He'd do it even it were *Godzilla vs. the Martians.*

Rigg felt a light touch on his shoulder and turned to see Sophie standing there. She was wearing scrub bottoms and a T-shirt with nothing underneath. He put his arm out, pulled her toward him, and nuzzled her breasts through the filmy fabric.

He looked up. "Sit here." Rigg patted the flat spot on the rock beside him.

"It's a beautiful sunrise," Sophie said.

"I finally understand why you are so fond of them," he said.

"I didn't like waking up without you," she said.

"I was restless."

In the sky, the oranges were bursting into blue.

"Is something wrong?" Sophie asked.

Rigg put his arm around Sophie, mainly because he was afraid that if he weren't holding her in place, she'd get up and run as soon as he told her about the film in Australia.

"I probably should have said something last night. Nicola offered me an opportunity to direct an independent film."

"That's wonderful. It's what you wanted," Sophie said.

"Their director fell out at the last minute. It's a fantastic opportunity. There's only one catch."

"You have to sleep with Nicola."

"Don't be stupid."

"Well, she's a movie star."

"To me, she's just Nicola Upton, a girl I've known since university."

"That may be worse."

"You're not making sense."

"Men always say that when they don't understand what you are saying." She was looking at her bare feet.

"None of this could have happened without you," he said, turning toward her. "Look at me." She gazed up at him for a moment before turning away.

"Why do you say that?"

"You made me stop being such a knob."

"Is that *knob,* with or without a *K?*"

It took a minute for him to understand what she was saying. "With a *K.* Tip of the penis *knob,* pain in the bottom—that kind of *knob.*"

"So, what is the catch, then?" she asked.

"I have to leave today for Melbourne. I won't be coming back to LA with you."

Chapter 22

THIS LOVE THING isn't worth it. Just when you think you have it all figured out, it sneaks up behind you and whacks you on the head with a two-by-four. I had never been given to wide mood swings—ecstasy one minute and despair the next. Even so, now I was hanging onto a racing roller coaster with the tips of my fingers.

From everything I've seen and read, these early stages of being in love are supposed to be obsessive; you can't keep your hands off each other. It's that sweetness you return to again and again as real life wanders in. Last night was like that—and this morning, when Rigg rested his head between my breasts—but the next moment, he told me he was leaving.

Too soon. I had already been picturing exchanging Christmas presents. I was going to get him a vest like mine. I was dying to see his reaction. Of course, I'd get him something else, too, something that he'd actually like. Then, there was New Year's Eve to think about, and I wanted, just for once in my life, to turn to the man I loved at the stroke of midnight and have a nice long kiss. Instead, Halley and I would probably do what we usually did. At around midnight, we went down to the billboard on Santa Monica Boulevard that tallied, in real time, how many people died from smoking. Don't laugh. We are never the only ones there.

I don't know how a few days could bloat me with expectation, but they had. And now Rigg had deflated me.

At least I could hold my head high, knowing that I behaved with grace and dignity, for the most part anyway. I think I hid my feelings pretty well under the circumstances. In fact, I was downright admirable.

Today, we had that glorious sunrise as background. I hope Rigg Greensman hasn't managed to taint mornings for me.

He says I changed him, which may or may not be true. I have to admit that he helped me get out of my own way. He loosened me up and encouraged my jokes. I know I am the better for it. Still, I feel cheated. I can't blame Rigg for doing what any rational person would do in his situation. I just hope he hasn't transferred that mega-chip on his shoulder to me. I don't want to be distorted by a big old block of pain and resentment.

Playing the recorder usually helps. That's why I took it up in the first place. I was a nervous kid, and the school therapist suggested I do something musical. Now, I think I might be asking for more than what a simple wind instrument can deliver.

I don't want to play anything too dreary. If I managed to keep my misery to myself out there on the rock, I don't have to lose my cool now. I choose "Always Look on the Bright Side of

Life" from the musical version of *Life of Brian*. You can never go wrong with Monty Python. I play around with that tune and hope that if Rigg can hear me, he won't miss the tone of cheerful resilience.

When the melody reached Rigg, he was still sitting outside on the rock feeling like a bastard. He knew he was doing what anyone else faced with this choice would do.

Monty Python. Rigg loved Monty Python—no—he *worshipped* Monty Python.

Sophie constantly surprised him. Nicola rarely did, but then again, he'd known her for such a long time. The idea of being surprised by Sophie every day for a very long time, maybe even the rest of his life, had a powerful appeal. Still, when he stacked up a brand-new love against an opportunity he'd been waiting for since he left university, he had to grab the opportunity. Who could blame him?

Rigg was pretty sure Nicola wanted him back and that this fact was at the bottom of her offer. And he knew it was the change in him that inspired it. Ironically, it was Sophie he had to thank for it.

Chapter 23

I HAD PICTURED the two of us flying back to Los Angeles together. The long plane ride would have been fun if I could have taken it with Rigg. What I had thought of as *my* project has become *our* project, and I wanted us both to be there when Corey West gave us his verdict.

It's hard to believe that a man who had initially brought out the absolute worst in me ended up bringing out not just the best in me but also more creativity than I thought I had. Before Rigg had come along, I hadn't seen myself as a terribly inventive person. But then Rigg convinced me to let down my hair—literally.

My dirty clothes get squished into the empty corners of my duffle. I fold the new things that we bought in Sharm el-Sheikh and place them carefully on top, leaving out something to wear on the plane. Normally, I'd wear scrubs because they're comfortable, even if I can be mistaken for someone who actually knows something about medicine. However, EMT-chic isn't the look I want Rigg to remember, and Ahmed is driving us both to the airport at the same time. The skinny jeans might be restrictive, but I want to dress so that Rigg will be eating his heart out when he gets on the plane that flies away from me.

Then again, I'm unconvinced that anything I wear will make that happen. There is nothing I can do to my appearance that will ensure my place in Rigg's heart. In a contest based only on looks, Nicola wins hands down. It's like she were custom designed by a doll maker specializing in big-eyed princesses.

I might have to accept the fact that what Rigg and I had was a fling, a burst of inspired energy gone astray. The next time I see him will probably be in *People* magazine. He'll be walking on the beach in Malibu with Nicola and their towheaded toddler.

There's a knock on the door to my room. I open it, and Rigg is standing outside.

"So now you knock," I say, smiling when I think of him catching me in the shower. I wish he'd make assurances, guarantees in writing and signed before a notary that what we have isn't over.

"I don't think we finished our conversation," he says.

"You have something more to say?" I turn and go back to my duffle bag where I pretend to pack. It requires taking out some things that I've already put in, but Rigg doesn't seem to notice. He steps behind me, and I can feel the heat coming off his body. It's as if he sucked up the warm sunlight and is reflecting it back on me.

"We got carried away. That's all," I say. "Together in an exotic location. I'll bet it happens all the time."

He puts his hands on my shoulders and turns me around so that I am facing him.

"I wouldn't call the Pigeon House an exotic location," he says.

"You know what I mean. The Sinai Peninsula—Egypt."

"Do you really think that's all it was? You think we just got carried away?"

I tilt my head to look up into his face. His gaze is expectant, and I probably shouldn't use this moment to bash his teeth in, but a girl has to protect herself.

"I do," I say.

He steps back as if I had actually struck him. "Oh, and the things we said to each other?"

"People say things in the heat of the moment."

He picks up my recorder from where it is lying on the bed. "I never thought I'd become so fond of a glorified whistle." He moves it around in his fingers.

"It's not a whistle. It's a treble recorder." I take it from him. When our fingers touch, it jolts electricity up my arm.

Rigg looks flustered, and I come close to telling him that everything I've just said is nonsense. But I can't. Too dangerous. I could fall apart. I could start weeping. If he thinks of me in the future, I don't want him to remember a puddle. I want him to summon up the girl who was free enough to make love between sand dunes.

"So, just to be clear. You didn't mean anything you said in the last few days?" he asks.

"I'm sure I meant some of it."

"You know what I mean."

"I think you should go to Australia without worrying about anything you said to me."

"Do you care what I think?"

"Of course."

"I think you don't trust me."

"That's incredibly unfair," I say. But he's right. I don't trust him. If I did, I wouldn't need to be so self-protective.

In the lobby, Katya pulls out my paperwork. I go over to the counter and sign it. We came in under budget, so Discovery won't have any complaints.

"Thank you for everything you did for me, Katya."

"It was fun. I felt like a fairy godmother."

"Well, it's after midnight."

"Why do you say that?"

"Rigg isn't coming back to LA with me. He's going to Australia to direct a movie."

"That doesn't mean anything."

"He's doing it with his old girlfriend."

"So what?"

"So, she's a movie star."

Katya shrugs, but looks a little less sure. "Did you tell Rigg how you feel?"

"I don't even know how I feel. I never do."

"Of course you know how you feel, and you should tell him."

I shake my head. "You're the one who said that trying to control a man can never work."

She presses her lips together. "I told you that chasing a man doesn't work. I didn't tell you to drive him away." She comes out from the back of the counter and gives me a brief hug. "Tell him how you feel."

"It's too late."

Rigg comes in a few minutes later, rucksack on one shoulder and carrying his duffle. He has a script tucked under his arm. He looks happy. And as much as I hate to admit it, that breaks my heart.

Chapter 24

OUTSIDE, RIGG HOISTS my bag into the trunk (he calls it the "boot") and opens the front door for me. This time, I wish I were relegated to the backseat, so I could just sit there in silence. You don't feel as much of an obligation to talk when you're sitting alone in the back.

Rigg gets into the back, and Ahmed pulls out of the parking lot.

"Sophie," Ahmed says, "I will ask you one more time. Will you be my wife and take me home to California with you?"

I am not in the mood for this. "Yes, Ahmed. I think it's a very good idea."

He is so surprised, he takes his foot off the gas, and the car behind us lays on its horn. "You are fooling with me," Ahmed says, turning his eyes back to the road. He is smiling, so I know I haven't hurt his feelings. There is a part of him, no doubt, that wants to go to America, and maybe he'll find the right woman to help him get there, but he's known all along it isn't me. This teasing is just part of his routine.

"In any case, Sophie's taken," Rigg says. I turn around so fast, I almost snap my neck. I'm not sure if I heard right. Maybe he said, "I'm taking Sophie's suitcase." Neither makes much sense. I know which sentence I hope he said, but it's not like I can ask him to repeat it.

Chapter 25

RIGG PULLS MY bag from the trunk and offers to carry it. He may have turned into Mr. Chivalry, but it's probably safer now to think about him the way he was before: obstreperous, uncooperative, and self-involved.

"No one has to carry it; it's on wheels," I say, taking the handle.

"You don't have to insist on being so damned independent all the time."

"Actually, I do. That's who I am and there's no reason to change it."

At the airport entrance, we check the departure screen. It's a small airport, but we are leaving from different ends. We stand in the middle of the lobby. People ebb and flow around us, but it is as if we were the only ones there.

Rigg puts his bags down and pulls me into a strong hug. I breathe in his clean toasty scent. "Have a safe flight, Bird Nerd." He says *Bird Nerd* like an endearment. Rigg leans down and kisses me. His lips are chapped from the desert wind. I want to remember what they feel like. He explores my mouth with his tongue, not like last night, but with hesitance, as if the kiss is asking a question.

I want to stay here forever.

I can't stand another minute of this.

"I'll call you when I'm back in LA," he says as he pulls away. He is looking over my left shoulder. My stomach sinks. He's not going to call until he gets back to California? We are in the world of cell phones, Skype, and WhatsApp. I suppose the time difference could be tricky. Maybe he'll be too absorbed in his movie to think of anything else. He certainly won't need a distraction. Even though it all makes sense, it feels like the brush-off I've been expecting. The issue of trust is sitting between us like a big fat elephant.

"A lot can happen between now and then. I could marry Ahmed," I say. Rigg doesn't laugh. He touches my cheek.

I turn then and walk away, dragging my bag behind me. I haven't gone far when I stop and turn to look at Rigg. He's still standing where I left him. I drop my duffle and run back. He scoops me into his arms. If this is going to be our last moment together, I want it to count for something. I want to be able to take out this memory and polish it up now and then.

I pull back and smile. "No matter what happens, we'll always have the Pigeon House," I say.

"It ain't exactly Paris," he says in a bad American accent.

"Here's looking at you, kid." I try to make this sound funny. And though I know the problems of two little people don't amount to a hill of beans, at the moment, they feel like they do.

"You are something else." He shakes his head ruefully.

"And don't you forget it." I give him the kind of smile I hope will stick with him.

Then, I turn to retrieve my bag from the floor. I walk toward my gate without looking back.

Chapter 26

MY MOTHER IS there to pick me up at LAX. She always comes in and waits at the gate, never sits in the car at the curb. Today she has a red balloon. It's because of the French film *Le Ballon Rouge*. A balloon follows a little boy all over Paris. We watched the movie when I was small, and from then on, a very round, very red balloon became Mom's way of telling me she loves me and I'll never be alone.

She opens her arms to me, and I step into them. I'm home. My mother smells like Jo Malone's White Jasmine and Mint cologne. She is wearing her usual crisp button-down blouse, a blazer, skinny jeans, and pumps. Her hair is newly cut and colored. I can see that she's had more high-lights put in. She has brown hair, but she always says that she's a natural blonde at heart. She is also wearing her sig-nature strings of pearls and an Hermès scarf, a gift from one of her wealthy regular customers.

We wait for my bag to come around the carousel. I grab it, and we walk out into the scrum of the airport. The honking cars. The air heavy with fumes. The red balloon bobs beside us and people look at us as we go by.

"You look tired, but that outfit…it's fantastic." Mom says.

"It was a long flight," I say. "But thanks."

"I was hoping you'd be exhilarated."

"I can be exhilarated after a good night's sleep."

"Fair enough."

I stow my Patagonia in the trunk and get into the car. We maneuver our way out of the crowded airport. My mother honks her horn to keep an enormous white Lexus from sideswiping us. She rolls down the window. "Stop texting, idiot. You've got kids in the car."

It's unlikely that the driver can hear anything in that climate-controlled monster vehicle. My mother drives a Chevy Volt, and my Smart car is electric. We try to do what we can for the environment. My mother could probably afford a bigger car now that she has become successful and my college and graduate school tuition is a thing of the past, but Mom says the idea of big things being better is a conceit of the new millennium.

When Mom drops me off at my one-bedroom apartment in North Hollywood, I haul my bag upstairs to the second floor and tie the balloon to a dining room chair.

Halley comes over after work to welcome me home. She brings Thai food since my cupboard is bare.

"Nice balloon," Halley says. "I wish my mother did things like that."

"I'm lucky. I know."

"That's what I like about you. You don't take anything for granted. Even though it's just been the two of you all these years, you think you're lucky."

"I know I am." I pull the containers out of the paper bag and put them on a tray with some silverware and a couple of plates. "You want a beer?"

"I wouldn't say no. It was a long day."

I don't drink too much at home so a couple of six packs last a long time on the bottom shelf of my refrigerator. I pull out two bottles and open them. Then, I sit on the chair that's anchoring the balloon and Halley sits kitty-corner to me.

"So, give me all the buzz," Halley says.

"I loved it. I never thought I could love doing something so much. And I have you to thank for it. I wish you'd been there." I hand the pad Thai over to Halley so she can help herself. She's a vegetarian, too. One of the ways we are super compatible.

"I got to stay home and do the really exciting stuff like talking to a bunch of weirdos about their lunatic ideas for new projects."

"But you love it."

"I really do," she admits, handing over the carton. Tell me about your new look. Don't you usually travel in scrubs?"

"What new look?" I tease. I hide a smile by shoving noodles into my mouth.

"You left looking like a refugee from an L.L.Bean catalog, and you came back looking like you walked out of a photo spread for *Destinations'* luxury camping issue."

"Rigg suggested these changes when he put me on camera."

"So, how was he? He's got an awful rep."

"Did you know that before you sent him?"

"Technically, it was Corey who sent him. And I didn't say anything because I didn't want to prejudice you against Rigg before you met him. What was he like? I hear he's hot."

"He is handsome."

"But that's so not your type."

"I know. I've always been wary of drop-dead gorgeous." I laugh and a piece of peanut flies out of my mouth and lands across the table.

"Oh, my God. Something happened between you," she says trying to get me to meet her eye. I shrug and bite my bottom lip. "I thought he's been with Nicola Upton for years," she adds.

"On and off." I shove a big forkful of noodles into my mouth so I can pretend I'm too busy chewing to talk. I don't think I'm ready to spill everything yet, not even to Halley.

"I've seen some of the footage you sent. You are so good in it. I couldn't believe the way you told all those stories, making the birds into characters. I never would have thought of it. I'm glad you didn't worry about some scientists thinking that it wasn't a serious approach."

"I've always anthropomorphized the birds in my head. When I realized that I could use that to bring in a bigger audience, the lighter, more entertaining approach suddenly made perfect sense. And I have Rigg to thank."

Chapter 27

I AM SITTING on the Bevel sofa in Corey West's office, and he, strangely, is walking on a treadmill in the corner while talking to me.

"You've done a great job, Sophie. Better than I ever could have expected. The way you've made yourself into a character was magical. My boss thinks this could be another *Naked and Afraid*. You could be the Anthony Bourdain of birds. I shit you not. You've turned out to be a spunky on-air personality. You are so photogenic and frankly, it was a surprise. I knew Rigg might try to sneak on camera. He's such a ham and looks good on anything. He is English eye candy, a blond Ioan Gruffudd."

"Who is Ioan Gruffudd?"

"He was in that show where he played an immortal in New York City. That guy could make any woman squirm."

"I had no idea you were such a romantic," I say.

"And as for you, you turned out to be hot. Man, why were you hiding it? If we weren't working together, I'd definitely date you."

"I'm never sure if you're sexually harassing me. How do you manage it?"

"I know the line and I don't go over it. I might snuggle up close to it, but I never step across."

"There you go again."

"Everyone has their special genius. That just happens to be mine."

You'd think such a cocky guy might be the slightest bit attractive, but Corey West looks like a Kewpie doll: short, pudgy, and bald, except for a patch of hair at the top that he could turn into a mohawk if he used enough hair product.

He turns off the treadmill, and it grinds to a halt.

"Fifteen minutes three times a day," he says.

I guess that's how much he thinks he needs to walk to maintain his below-par physique.

"Well, it shows." I take a breath and try not to laugh.

He comes over and sits on the chair beside me. "I have good news for you. Very good news," he says. I wait. I'm tempted to move a few inches away because Corey's a space invader. A sweaty scent is emanating from him. Corey is mercurial in an odd way. He's thoroughly charming one minute and horribly obnoxious the next. Halley told me this is pretty common among entertainment types. He leans in toward me. "We want to offer you a series."

"I don't understand."

"Honestly, we thought this was going to be a one-off. A nice little bird documentary about migration. It filled a niche. Your friend Halley was pushing for you, so we decided to give you a shot. We never thought you'd do something so interesting and engaging with it."

"Thank you," I say, trying not to feel insulted by his low expectations. I stand, partly to get away from Corey and partly because I can't sit still. I am either excited or terrified, and I can't tell which.

"Since you focused so much on the mating instead of the migration, we want to call the show either *Bird Nerd* or *The Mating Season*. Jury's still out on that. Of course, you'll need to get Rigg on board," he says. "And time is of the essence. We have a certain slot to fill, and we're going to need you in Madagascar in two weeks."

"I've always wanted to go to Madagascar." I sit in a guest chair on the other side of the coffee table. "What if there is no Rigg?" I ask.

"I thought the two of you started to get along. It shows in the video."

Nodding, I tell him, "We got along all right in the end. That's not the problem."

"Then, what is it?"

"He's in Australia. I guess he didn't tell you."

"The project is complete. He doesn't have to check in with me. What's he doing there?"

"A movie with his friends from university."

"Does that mean he's working with Philip Piggott-Barnes?"

"And Nicola Upton and Simon Marsten."

"Great opportunity for him."

"And bad break for us," I sighed. "Can't we do it with someone else?"

Corey shakes his head. "No way. The chemistry between you is the magic ingredient. It has to be you and Rigg or there is no show. Rigg's charisma, paired with your quirkiness, that's what made this unique. Without that, it's just another bird doc."

I can hardly bring myself to choke out the words. "Then, I guess there's no show."

"We could try to reach him," Corey says, helpfully.

"If you were Rigg and had to choose between doing a feature film with your famous friends and a bird show, which would you choose?"

Corey shrugs, and I notice that he doesn't have much in the way of shoulders. He takes a glass of water from a carafe on his desk. "You want anything?"

"Anything that will make me forget that I just got and lost an amazing opportunity in the span of two minutes."

"I've got vodka in the mini fridge."

"It's okay. I probably shouldn't drown my sorrows just yet. I have to drive home."

Every day since I've been back, I've scanned the internet for news about Rigg. I usually type in "Nicola Upton" first. There isn't much. It's like they've fallen off the face of the earth. I try to keep myself from picturing the day I'll come across an announcement that the lovebirds are together again. There will be a picture of them, heads bowed toward each other, billing and cooing. Just thinking about it gives me a pain in my chest.

How could I have been so stupid? I turned a fling into something more. I wanted it to be permanent, whatever that means. Just like my mother expected her marriage to my father to be permanent. She never expected that he'd walk across the street one day and be gone forever.

Rigg and I live in different ecospheres. My connection to entertainment is tangential to say the least, but to Rigg, entertainment is the whole world. He wants a type of success I don't dream about and don't care about. Even now, though I am disappointed for myself, I am thinking about all the good I could have done with a show that subtly influences people to take care of the planet. I could have done something really meaningful.

Chapter 28

MY DOORBELL IS ringing. In fact, someone is leaning on it. I look at the clock. It's eleven o'clock in the morning and though the sun is shining through my open curtains, it wasn't enough to wake me.

I get up and stumble to the front door. I press my eye to the spy hole. My mother is standing on the other side of it holding a bag. I unlatch the chain lock and swing the door open.

"Time to get on with your life," she says. "You've been lounging around here long enough. And you need to get out of those purple scrubs. You look like a bruise. I would have opened up and come in with my key, but you have that chain that is more likely to keep out intrusive mothers than actual criminals." She walks toward my kitchen and starts to unload the bag. "I brought bagels, coffee, and some staples. Have you even been out since you got back?"

I follow her into the kitchen and sit on a stool on one side of the butcher block partition that separates the kitchen from the dining area. I have been wearing the same purple scrubs for three days and nights. I don't think they've started to stink yet, but I'm not the best judge of that. In any case, I'm probably at the edge of the envelope.

"I've only been back for four days," I say. "I've been having most of my stuff delivered."

"You could have called me."

"No need. I was tired. That's all. Before you rang the bell, I was dreaming that I went to the doctor, and they said that something was wrong with my heart, and I had to go directly to the emergency room or I could die. Should I make an appointment with Dr. Glanzman?"

Mom pulls out a bag of coffee beans and then bends to get my electric grinder from the cabinet. "Dreams aren't literal. You know that. If I were to interpret that dream though, I'd say you were brokenhearted. And I don't know why that would be, do you?" She straightens up, pours some beans into the grinder, and presses the button. That machine makes such an awful noise, I wonder if fresh coffee is really worth it.

The word *brokenhearted* makes me want to cry. Or maybe it's the way she homed in on my feelings like a heat-seeking missile.

"Would you like to tell me what happened?" she asked. "Didn't the Discovery Channel like what you did?"

"They loved it."

"Then why are you moping around like you lost your best friend?" she asks. When I don't speak, she says, "Ah. It's a man."

I nod and chew on my bottom lip. "I think I'm in love."

"I'm sorry," she says. "That's really too bad."

Her answer is so unexpected it makes me laugh. "Why would you say that?"

"In my experience, love has much in common with mental illness."

"That's so cynical. You loved Dad, didn't you?'

"Very much. Now get dressed," she says. "I should have brought a bottle of Febreze with me. I suggest you get some to spray around in here."

"That bad?" I ask.

"I'm afraid so."

After I've showered, I go back to the kitchen. I've exchanged my purple scrubs for jeans and a white T-shirt. Mom has toasted some bagels and put a spread on the table, complete with cream cheese, peanut butter, coffee, and orange juice.

"Now I know what's wrong with you. You are all twisted up with love. And the unrequited kind, or you wouldn't be so upset," Mom says.

"Not exactly. We requited quite a bit." I give her a mischievous smile.

"Who was he?"

"Rigg, my cameraman."

"That's his name?"

"Riggan. He's English."

"I'm not sure that's an excuse," Mom says. She picks up a bagel and layers it with cream cheese.

"So, what happened?"

"He went to direct a movie in Australia with his old girl-friend who just happens to be Nicola Upton."

"The actress?"

"The movie star."

"So, you think it's over between you?"

I take a sip of coffee. My mother makes great coffee. "He hasn't tried to contact me. Which is troubling because they have phones in Australia and the internet, too—or so I've been told."

"Have you tried to contact him?"

"You can't force someone to love you. He knows how I feel."

"Are you sure?"

"Positive."

"Only fools are positive," she says.

"Are you sure?"

"Positive."

This is a routine we've been going through since I was little. I think it's from the Three Stooges. After I tell my mother about the potential series that was offered and then snatched away almost simultaneously, she decides we need to go out and have some fun.

We go to Venice Beach where we stroll the boardwalk with all the tourists and lunatics. I always look for Harry Perry, the Kama Kosmic Krusader, who's been skating on the boardwalk with an electric guitar and a turban for forty years. Mom finds him annoying. She says he's created a brand out of being weird, but I like him. I like his eccentricity, even if it is pretend. It relaxes me.

We stop at the table of a psychic named Clara Voyant. Mom thinks this is hysterical and insists on getting readings.

Ms. Voyant is blond and slim. She looks more like a shampoo model than a psychic.

"You will meet a man," she says to me.

"That's a pretty safe bet," I say, turned off by how wrong she is already.

"He will be very short."

I am tempted to say, "Wrong again," but I keep my mouth shut. My mother frowns.

Clara Voyant is so off base, she isn't even entertaining. It's fun to see how well a stranger can read you, but it's clear Clara is no intuitive. We give up on her quickly, hand her a few bucks, and leave without looking back.

"I can read people better than she can," I say as we walk away. "And I'm hardly brilliant at it."

"Can you?" Mom asks.

"If you mean Rigg, then maybe not."

"You don't have that much experience with men."

"There was Johnson Pinkwater."

"As I said, not much experience. Come on. Let's get our names written on a grain of rice. We haven't done that in ages."

After we leave the beach, we stop at a boutique on Main Street where Mom knows the proprietor.

"Now that you're open to it, I thought we could pick up a few things," Mom says.

"I don't need anything."

"If you can let a man you hardly know change your whole look, you can give me a chance. I've been waiting years for this."

My poor mother has spent my life stepping back to allow me my independence. The least I can do is give in to her. Maybe I should have done it long ago. I try on five pairs of pants and don't make one complaint. My mother chooses the three she likes best. I don't whine about fashion being a waste of time and money. I don't tell her I want to be judged by my brains, not my looks. I realize that I have been so ungenerous with her, and she has been so generous with me. I was so busy being my own person, I never stopped to think that being a little flexible wouldn't kill me and it might give her a little joy. I have Rigg to thank for this: he got me to stop taking myself so seriously.

We stop on Rose Avenue for dinner at Café Gratitude. It's a favorite of mine, because it's vegan and delicious. I order *I Am Humble,* an Indian curry. Rigg would probably choose the *I Am Awesome* panini. Maybe that's not fair; there is more to him that that. He could order the *I Am Warmhearted* and I wouldn't bat an eye.

On Sunday morning, I wake with the dawn. It's my TreePeople day. Halley and I volunteer in the morning and usually go out for lunch afterward. I pick one of my new outfits and look at myself in the mirror. I look thinner when I'm not wearing clothes that are at least two sizes too big for me.

I have forgotten to put my safari vest in the dryer so I won't be able to wear it today. I tug on a cotton sweater and fill up a leather backpack my mother gave me.

The day with my mom had cheered me up. My relationship (or lack thereof) with Rigg wasn't the only thing to be upset about. That had been a blow, but I had also come so close to reaching a lot of people, to letting them know how important it is to protect the biosphere, too. I had plenty to be disappointed about, but getting back to my routine was the best thing for it.

I drive my electric car east on Ventura and then south on Coldwater Canyon until I reach the top and pull into the lot at TreePeople. I meet my group of eight-year-olds. They are here for their first bird walk—a program that Halley and I created because we had such a positive experience as the only kids. It is a lucky morning. We see a red-tailed hawk, two hummingbirds, and a warbler. An hour in, and the kids are already getting tired. Not every child takes to birding the way I did.

We are on our way back to the trailhead. I am trying to get the children to repeat the names of the birds and some of the plants we've seen. When I'm with the kids, my focus is laser sharp. I look up and see someone walking our way, and it's as if I'm being awakened from a trance. The figure is speckled in the shadows of the sycamore leaves and it take a few seconds for me to register who I'm seeing.

But there he is.

Rigg.

At first, I think I may be imagining things—my wishful thinking has conjured him up out of thin air. As he moves toward us, there is no doubt of his solidity. If he were a mirage, I'd be able to see through him, but he's as solid as the trees around us.

I reach out and touch him just to be sure. The children can tell that something odd is happening, and they begin to titter like sparrows. At first, I just stand there, too shocked to move or to speak. Halley and her group of little birders enter the clearing where we are standing. "Kids," she says to my group, "you'll be joining us. I'll walk you all back to the parking lot to meet your parents." Halley and all the children go off in one direction and Rigg and I walk in the other, toward a bower and a rough-hewn bench. We sit down, and he takes my hand in both of his. I can feel that broken heart of mine slowly mending.

"What are you doing here?" I ask.

"Your mother told me where to find you."

"But you're supposed to be in Australia," I say dumbly.

"Apparently not."

"Why not?"

"Corey tracked me down."

"You gave up a feature film with a major movie star to do a bird show with me?"

"That's about the size of it."

"That's crazy. You know that, don't you?"

"What can I say? You make me a little crazy." He lets go of my hands and shrugs his broad shoulders. He looks like a twelve-year-old boy about to ask a girl to a school dance.

"But why did you choose the birds?"

"Someone once told me that there are things more important than fame and glory."

"Whoever said that needs to have her head examined." I laugh. He pulls me in and the kiss we share is so sweet it tastes like candy.

"And I didn't choose the birds," he says when he breaks away.

"You didn't?"

"I chose you."

Epilogue

WESLEY ALAMIEYESEIGHA IS scheduled to meet a couple at Ivato International Airport in Antananarivo and drop them at the Anjajavy Nature Reserve. He often picks up rich tourists and takes them to the Lodge. When he sees all the stuff this couple is carrying, he is immediately concerned. Despite their matching safari vests, they do not look like outdoor types—especially not the man, who looks like a film star. The young woman is pretty with long hair the color of honey fresh from the honeycomb.

"You might want to try one of the resort hotels instead," Wesley tentatively suggests.

"Maybe after we are finished, we'll take a few extra days," the man says. His name, according to the itinerary Wesley has been given, is Rigg Greensman.

"Finished with what?" Wesley asks.

"We are shooting footage of birds for a television series," the woman, Sophie Castle, says. "Madagascar is supposed to be a unique place for it."

"I once flew Mr. Leonardo DiCaprio to the reserve." The couple does not react. They, too, are from Hollywood. Maybe they know Mr. DiCaprio, so for them this is not impressive.

"We're filming the mating habits of birds," Rigg says. "Sophie is an ornithologist."

Sophie gets all pink around the ears. Rigg throws an arm around her, and her whole face goes scarlet. Strange for a scientist to get all disconcerted when she hears the word *mating*. Wesley does not believe this woman is thinking about birds. She looks at the man like she wants to gobble him up.

Once all the gear is stowed, they take off into a cloudless sky. No matter how many times Wesley flies over the lush forests and azure water, he never tires of the view. The engine of the Cessna Skyhawk is so loud, it's impossible to speak over all the noise.

He guides the plane smoothly onto the landing strip. When Wesley kills the engine, there is a moment of preternatural quiet. Then, as usual, Wesley's ears adjust to the chirps and buzz of birds and insects.

They unload the backpacks, tent, water filter, food, cameras, power source, and anything else two people might need for a week alone in the wild. It's a lot of stuff, but they claim that their campsite is nearby, no more than a mile. In addition to their packs, they each have a collapsible camp wagon. Once everything is on the ground, Wesley looks at the couple skeptically. "Are you going to be all right?" he asks.

"We'll be fine," Sophie says. A tropical breeze blows a few

strands of hair across her face and Rigg sweeps them back with a gentle hand.

"Better than fine," he says, stroking Sophie's long hair.

Wesley is reluctant to leave them, though he has to assume they know what they're doing. Either that or they are so in love, they've lost their minds and aren't thinking clearly. Still, Wesley would feel more comfortable if the van from the Lodge were there to greet them. "Okay, then. Good luck," Wesley says as he hoists himself back into the cockpit.

As he pulls out, he looks back. The couple is waving. Two happy people in matching safari vests. Those vests are not attractive, Wesley thinks, but they are probably very handy.

Can a little black dress change everything?

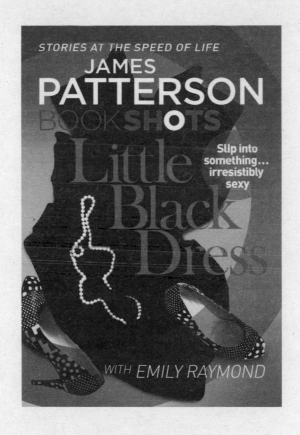

Read on for an extract

IN THE OPULENT LIMESTONE lobby of the Four Seasons New York, I handed over my Amex. "A city-view king, please." No tremor in my voice at all. Nothing to betray the pounding of my heart, the adrenaline flooding my veins.

Am I really about to do this?

Maybe I should have had another glass of rosé.

The desk clerk tapped quickly on her keyboard. "We have a room on the fortieth floor," she said. "Where are you two visiting from?"

I shot a glance over my shoulder. *Honestly? About twenty-five blocks from here.* My knees were turning into Jell-O.

Behind me, Michael Bishop, a thumb hooked in the belt loop of his jeans, flashed his gorgeous smile—first at me, then at the clerk. "Ohio, miss," he said, giving his muscled shoulders an aw-shucks shrug. His eyes were green as jade. "Mighty big city you got here, darlin'," he said, a drawl slipping into his voice.

"Oh—Ohio," the clerk repeated, like it was the most beautiful word she'd ever heard. She looked like she was unbuttoning his shirt with her eyes as she handed me the room key.

Very unprofessional, if you ask me.

But then again, how professional was it to check into a hotel with one of *Metropolitan*'s freelance writers—who, by the way, had obviously never even *been* to Ohio?

If he had, he'd have known they don't talk like cowboys there.

Michael Bishop lived on the Lower East Side of Manhattan; I lived on the Upper West Side. We'd known each other since our first years in the magazine business. Today we'd met for lunch, to go over a story he was writing for *Metropolitan*. The café, an elegant little French place with fantastic *jambon beurre* sandwiches, was close to my office.

It was also close to the Four Seasons.

We'd laughed, we'd had a glass of rosé—and now, suddenly, we were here.

Am I really about to do this?

"If you want tickets to a Broadway show or reservations at Rao's, the concierge can assist you," the clerk offered. By now she'd taken off Michael's shirt and was licking his chest.

"Actually," I said, "we have other plans." I grabbed Michael's hand and pulled him into the elevator before I lost my nerve.

We stood in front of our reflections in the gold-mirrored doors. "Really?" I said to mirror-Michael, who was as gorgeous as the real Michael but yellower. *"Ohio?"*

He laughed. "I know, Jane—you're a former fact-checker, so the truth is very important to you," he said. "I, however, am a writer, and I take occasional *liberties* with it." He stepped closer to me, and then he slipped an arm around my waist. "Nice dress, by the way," he said.

"Do you also take occasional liberties with your editors?" I asked, trying to be playful.

He shook his head. "Never," he said.

I believed him—but it didn't matter either way. This had been *my* idea.

It wasn't about loneliness, or even simple lust (though that obviously played a part). I just wanted to know if I could do something like this without feeling weird or cheap.

I still wasn't sure.

The hotel room was a gleaming, cream-colored box of understated luxury. A bottle of Chardonnay waited in a silver wine bucket, and there were gourmet chocolates arranged on the pillows. Through the giant windows, Manhattan glittered, a spectacle of steel and glass.

I stood in the center of the beautiful room, holding my purse against my body like a kind of shield. I was charged and excited and—all of a sudden—a little bit scared.

This was new territory for me. If I didn't turn tail and run right now, I was about to do something I'd barely even had the guts to imagine.

Michael, his green eyes both gentle and hungry, took the purse from my hands and placed it on a chair. Straightening up again, he brushed my hair away from my neck, and then he kissed me, gently, right above my collarbone. A shiver ran down my spine.

"Is this okay?" he asked softly.

I remembered the way he'd kissed my fingers at the café. I remembered how I'd said to him, *Let's get out of here.*

I wanted this.

"Yes," I breathed. "It's more than okay."

His lips moved up my neck, his tongue touching my skin ever so lightly. He traced a finger along my jawline and then slowly drew it down again, stopping at the low neckline of the Dress.

I waited, trembling, for him to slip his hand inside the silk.

But he didn't. He paused, barely breathing. And then he reached around my back and found the slender zipper between my shoulder blades. He gave it a sharp tug, and the black silk slid down my body in a whisper. I stood there— exposed, breathless, thrilled—and then Michael crushed his lips to mine.

We kissed deeply. Hungrily. I ran my palms up his strong arms, his broad shoulders. He reached under me and lifted me up, and I wrapped my legs around his waist. He tasted like wine.

I whispered my command: *"Take me to bed."* Then I added, "Please."

"So polite," he murmured into my hair. "Anything you say, Jane."

He carried me to the giant bed and laid me down on it. His fingers found my nipples through the lace of my bra, and then my bra, too, seemed to slip off my body, and his mouth was where his fingers had been.

I gasped.

Yes, oh yes. I'm really doing this.

His tongue teased me, pulled at me. His hands seemed to be everywhere at once. "Should I—" he began.

I said, "Don't talk, just do." I did not add *Please* this time.

I wriggled out of my panties as he undressed, and then he was naked before me, golden in the noon light, looking like some kind of Greek demigod descended from Mount Olympus.

I stretched up my arms and Michael fell into them. He kissed me again as I arched to meet him. When he thrust himself inside me, I cried out, rocking against his hips, kissing his shoulder, his neck, his chin. I pulled him into me with all my strength as the heat inside me rose in waves. When I cried out in release, my nails dug into Michael's shoulders. A moment later he cried out too, and then he collapsed on top of me, panting.

I couldn't believe it. I'd really done it.

Spent, we both slept for a little while. When I awoke, Michael was standing at the end of the bed, his shirt half buttoned, his golden chest still visible. A smile broke over his gorgeous face.

"Jane Avery, that was an incredible lunch," Michael Bishop said. "Could I interest you in dinner?"

I smiled back at him from the tangle of ivory sheets. As perfect as he was, as *this* had been, today was a one-time deal. I wasn't ready to get involved again. "Actually," I said, "thank you, but I have other plans."

He looked surprised. A guy like Michael wasn't used to being turned down. "Okay," he said after a moment. "I get it."

I doubted that he did.

It's not you, I thought, *it's me.*

After he kissed me good-bye—sweetly, longingly—I turned on the water in the deep porcelain tub. I'd paid seven hundred dollars for this room and I might as well enjoy it a little longer.

I sank into the bath, luxuriant with lavender-scented bubbles. It was crazy, what I'd done. But I'd loved it.

And I didn't feel cheap. *Au contraire:* I felt *rich*.

JAMES PATTERSON

BOOK**SHOTS**

OUT THIS MONTH

113 MINUTES

Molly Rourke's son has been murdered . . . and she knows who's responsible. Now she's taking the law into her own hands.

THE VERDICT

A billionaire businessman is on trial for violently attacking a woman in her bed. No one is prepared for the terrifying consequences of the verdict.

THE MATING SEASON

Sophie Castle has been given the opportunity of a lifetime: her own wildlife documentary. But her cameraman, Rigg Greensman, is unmotivated . . . and drop dead gorgeous.

TRUMP VS. CLINTON: IN THEIR OWN WORDS (ebook only)

Direct from the candidates, *Trump vs. Clinton* is an unvarnished conversation on the issues in this dramatic presidential election.

JAMES PATTERSON

BOOK**SHOTS**

COMING SOON

FRENCH KISS

French detective Luc Moncrief joined the NYPD for a fresh start – but someone wants to make his first big case his last.

$10,000,000 MARRIAGE PROPOSAL

A billboard offering $10 million to get married intrigues three single women in LA. But who is Mr. Right . . . and is he the perfect match for the lucky winner?

SACKING THE QUARTERBACK

Attorney Melissa St. James wins every case. Now, when she's up against football superstar Grayson Knight, her heart is on the line, too.

KILL OR BE KILLED

Four gripping thrillers – one killer collection. *The Trial, Little Black Dress, Heist* and *The Women's War*.

THE WOMEN'S WAR (ebook only)

Former Marine Corps colonel Amanda Collins and her lethal team of women warriors have vowed to avenge her family's murder.